EARTHQUAKE

A NOVEL BY *Milton Berle*

AND *John Roeburt*

EARTHQUAKE

Random House, New York

First Printing

To Ruth and Agda

. . . they felt the earth tremble under their feet. The sea swelled and foamed in the harbour, and beat to pieces the vessels riding at anchor. Whirlwinds of fire and ashes covered the streets and public places; houses fell, roofs were flung upon the pavements, and the pavements were scattered. Thirty thousand inhabitants of all ages and sexes were crushed under the ruins.

"What can be the *sufficient reason* of this phenomenon?" said Pangloss.

"This is the Last Day!" cried Candide.

EARTHQUAKE

Focus *was a fault plane within the earth more than one hundred miles long and three feet deep. With the sudden slip and breaking of rocks in the long fault, the earth telegraphed its warning to the observatories. Electronic fingers scrawled the phenomenon on paper strips for scientists to read. The paper strips ominously showed preliminary waves traveling outward in straight lines in all directions from* Focus, *at a velocity of six miles per second. And then secondary S waves, vibrating at right angles from* Focus, *slower in speed, but with more than twice the destructive power.*

The full force of the earthquake struck the highland slopes in which nestled the picturesque village of Choluca.

The surface of the ground rose in low, very swiftly moving waves, like those on water, upon the crest of which the soil opened in small cracks, closing again in wave troughs.

Flimsy wooden houses and poorly constructed, cheap mortar structures collapsed at once. Roads cracked open, and people and livestock fell into the earth. Water pipes and sewers broke, telephone poles vanished; the lovely waterways, which were so much the charm of Choluca, were clogged and choked with land fill and debris.

With the destruction came fire.

The earthquake was over surprisingly soon, for the incredible damage it did.

It lasted for a duration of exactly fifty-six seconds, less than a minute.

The fire raged on, spreading steadily, with few fire fighters and little equipment to curb and control it.

A reconnaissance helicopter, aloft over Choluca just after twilight, saw a huge flaming rose with its seed bank in deep Hell itself.

The after-shocks that were Hell's own telegraphy of disaster were now, with other communications broken, felt in the widest geographic arc:

On Mexico's Central Highway, a flat section of macadam tilted so that a driver momentarily lost the wheel.

On the steep slopes between Puebla and Cuernavaca, trees surged violently, like a field of ripe grain in the breeze.

On the sea floor in the Gulf of Mexico, a submarine cable was broken for the second time in fifty years.

Location shooting of an American TV adventure series stopped when a chartered boat in the Veracruz harbor listed and the Eclair camera fell to the sharks.

Over on the Pacific Ocean side, landslips in the green mountains of Acapulco sent dirt and stones rattling on the tiled roofs of the exotic town.

In the Guadalupe Sanctuary, while the poor prayed to the Virgin, a wall of the shrine formed cracks in the shape of a Cross.

A distance away, in an archaic cemetery bounding Xochicalco, a grave opened and exposed a figurine with eyes set with rubies.

This side of Cuautla, the volcano Popocatepetl, in a sudden lively moment, blew high puffs of flame at its snow lid.

In Mexico City, in the de luxe Del Prado Hotel, a waiter who couldn't keep his feet, balanced his fall so he did not drop his tray of cocktails.

In the Mayan ruins of Moxiquil, a commonwealth of ants wept over the million-hour cost of a fine metropolis of dwellings, redoubts, bridges, hospitals and food warehouses.

The time of the earthquake was exactly 6:54 P.M.

ing front showed him off even more favorably. It humanized Harding, made him *simpático*, frail as anybody.

There was a downgrade now, where the macadam lay as a valley between sheer hills. There were bulges on top—a natural symmetry that filled the senses with pictures of a gigantic, reclining nude. The colors were flame-green, bright orange, yellow and purple—a bouquet hot to the eye, baked in a tropical kiln by thousands of suns.

The chauffeur's eyes flirted, and a hand motioned excitedly. "Look quick, Señor Harding, and you will see a woman!"

Harding crooked a smile to Rufino, with no interest in it. His thoughts were on another tack, on a flesh-and-blood woman. On Susan, his wife, and the damned unending perplexities of his marriage. He swiftly made a correction in his mind now. *What had been his marriage.* There was an interlocutory decree now, for what uncontested Mexican divorces were worth. Susan was free, for the time anyhow; slipped through his fingers, out of his life.

Harding dried sweated palms on a handkerchief, then mopped his brow. The inner heat he felt was mainly annoyance, the feeling of being put out. He'd get her back, he was sure—drag her back bodily to Stamford. Anyhow, *coax* her back—Harding redecided his tactic. Play that well-grooved record about Sweethearts Forever in a cold, unfeeling world; bribe the neurotic bitch with cash, furs, a cute foreign car.

An old routine, and he was a practiced retriever. They'd played this same bit before, first in Arkansas, and after that in Reno.

His mind filled up with oaths now. *The goddam crap a man has to take . . .*

The road signs warned *peligro* and *curva*, and Rufino contrarily stamped down on the gas accelerator.

Harding yelled out, glad for a respite from his thinking, "Sonofabitch, pay attention to your driving!"

Rufino smiled with a gleam of gold teeth, and slowed the speed of the car. "You are too much too nervous, Señor Harding." He added soothingly, "You will surely find your wife in one of the inns in the village of Choluca."

Harding said edgily, "Like I was sure to find her at the Del Bosque in Mexico City!" The tic danced in his cheek. "If you climb on a carrousel, all you can expect to do is go around in circles." His face brooded. "Get to Choluca, I'll sure as hell be told she's in Acapulco!"

Rufino disputed it. "But we have reliable information that the Señora Harding is now a guest in one of the inns in Choluca." He grinned wisely and struck two fingers. "We have paid money to find this out."

"All right, *one* of the inns in Choluca," Harding said from between his teeth. "Meenie, minie, moe—how many damned inns do I have to canvass?"

"There is only two inns in Choluca." The chauffeur smiled goldenly. "Meanwhile, you must enjoy the beautiful scenery. Since you are anyhow here."

"Shove the beautiful scenery." Harding forced a smile. "No offense intended, Rufino. You're trying awfully to be a good scout, I know." He glanced briefly out the car window. "Sure, the scenery's beautiful—I can write a poem, count how many hills have teats. But I'm right now in no mood for it."

He dabbed the handkerchief at his brow again. "I've got counted hours; I left a mess of work behind. I flew in from New York, hoping to hell I could fly right out."

Rufino nodded compatibly. "Fly home *with* the Señora Harding." His face set grimly now, as if he was perhaps conjuring up a love-ache of his own. Soon the chauffeur sang-talked some phrases of an ancient song, slurring the words: " *'En una jaula de plata—se quejaba un pajarito— y en el quejido relata—de un modo muy exquisito—Dicen que el amor no mata—pero lastima un poquito.'* "

Rufino looked eagerly at Harding. When no request for a translation came, the chauffeur took his own initiative. "The sick bird in his cage says love only hurts him *poquito*, but will not kill him."

Harding smiled indulgently, as to the prattlings of a child. Rufino looked disappointed, then soon sought to blur his identification with the *yanqui's* marital miseries. Inner sight sought out his own, where she was—Rufino watched her at her daily tasks, competent as she was, and his eyes smiled in an outburst of pride and love. "*Más dichoso yo*"—I am the happiest. Rufino said it over and over superstitiously, then breathed in glad relief, twisting to shake his head pityingly at Harding.

Harding shifted in the wide seat and turned his back in an injunction against any further trespass or nuisance by the chauffeur. His mind was fretful now with the big stuff of his life, the *truer* crises; his inner eye scanning a paper trove of memoranda, graphs, charts, rating reports, his brain cannily kneading the bread of survival from the mealy verbs, nouns, postulations, glittering generalities of Agency Row.

As always before, the whirling audit of himself only produced its own special pain. The triumphs receded, blurred and erased—he stood pygmy-size in his mind's eye, snafued by coiling ribbons of tape that marked the endless records of his failures and mistakes.

He tried desperately now to project away from himself. *Don't be so damned subjective, so self-flogging!* He imaged his associates in Brant, Bellows, Appleby and Harding; stood Brant, Bellows and Appleby against one wall in the big Conference Room. He then ordered flannel-mouthed Zach Stachel and the Princeton prodigy Doobs into the line-up.

He had a quick, passing regret over Doobs. He'd been fond of the fellow once; they'd lunched together, gabbed, fished, tramped in the woods, helled around town nights. And then, suddenly, they'd stood on opposite sides of a wall of ice.

He now glared balefully at Stachel and Doobs, as if despising these two, paired, more than his formal associates in the agency. *Harpies*—show them a wound and they're right in there pecking at your flesh. One of them ever again patronizes me to impress Brant, or edits my ideas, damn me if I don't kick him right in the butt.

He looked darkly at the line-up again, individualizing them each in turn, while his electronic eye clicked its discovery of concealed metal.

Harding nodded calmly with the discovery, not one bit surprised over it. *Bellows's got a knife out for me;* also Appleby, Stachel and Doobs. We dropped five million in billings last year—Chesterfield switched, Chrysler got economy-complexed, Rector and Gumpel took their soap to another agency. Bellows has me tagged for scapegoat, to save his own face.

He now brought his summary wisdom to Appleby. Brant touted me into the firm, and Appleby's never forgiven that. Plus the fact that his drunken nympho wife won't get away from me at parties.

He wished Appleby dead now. *The next ulcer attack, I hope and pray the bastard bleeds to death.*

His stare fixed sternly on Stachel and Doobs; with a trick of the eye now, he saw them merged, as one face and body. They were identical, he told himself—the hair cropped close to the skull, the baby skin and sincere eyes; and lean and muscled in their uniform, gray suits.

The faggot look. Bet they've exchanged wedding rings, room together on the sly somewhere.

As anger flooded through Harding, he let his fancy run wild. He stood now as an Executioner confronting the line-up. He raised his tommy-gun, shot them all dead, then sprayed bullets into the fallen for that extra insurance. Except Brant. He left Brant standing unharmed.

I lose Brant, I'm in the soup. My one ace—I'm dead without Brant. Brant ever shuts down on me, I'm down at the emergency shelter begging for a flop. Brant's my guarantor with the bank, the finance companies. It's by grace of Brant I'm permitted to be in hock for more than fifty grand. I'm a credit risk, thanks to Brant.

Harding had a wincing afterthought now; his secret eye trained on a regimental line of mink. *I'm a triple-A credit risk in boudoirs too, thanks to Brant.*

Rufino completed a hairpin turn holding a mechanical lighter to the stub of a cigar. When the car was in equilibrium again, he grinned ear to ear over the bravado of his feat.

Harding tried hard to shut down on his thinking.

One worry at a time, mister. Right now, concentrate on Susan. Susan's why you're here in Mexico.

Let the harpies in the agency back in New York conspire, tear him to shreds in absentia. There was always another day, another round coming up.

Lose every battle, but win the final one.

Damn it to hell, where was the old moxie? Harding, the tough competitor; the wily in-fighter with *more* scalps in his trophy chest.

Blame it on taxes, the old h.c.l. You put tomorrow in hock to pay for yesterday.

Blame it on his father. Feed a kid with a gold spoon, and then go die five hundred dollars shy of the funeral costs.

Blame it on the analyst. He'd gone to consult about insomnia, and the s.o.b. had introduced him to neurosis. The year with Barshak had knocked the ego props from under him.

You can't keep to your feet with your rear on a couch.

Blame it on Susan. The perennial Vassar graduate. Still reaching for his hand in darkened theaters; hot stuff in parked cars. Playing waltz music as the background to candlelight suppers at home.

Always Juliet. Shocked dumb and frigid by four-letter words.

Comes this reuniting, he vowed, it's Susan who gets to park *her* ass on Barshak's couch. Be interesting to find out why she's so wild about romance, but lukewarm about sex.

He tried to reconjure her face now. But it blurred for him. He saw a woman's face, not too clearly Susan's, over the faces of the other women he'd known in these weeks since their bust-up. There were hazel eyes, spiraling brows, mascara, orange lip rouge—a blond head of hair that smelled of chemicals and smarted the nostrils. His eyes undressed her, seeking to fit from his memory stocks of breasts, bellies, thighs, bottoms, those attributes of Susan that were specially her own.

The trouble with modern woman—no individuality. Every one of them Look-Alikes with faces by Helena Rubenstein, rears by Slenderella, their blessed natural stink lost to Chanel and Lanvin.

He refurbished his last scene with Susan . . . but hard put to remember any of the dialogue. Susan on the graded driveway of their home, in the bright morning glare, with packed suitcases already stowed in the station wagon. In clothes and a hat he hadn't seen her in for a dozen years— as if these neglected garments were a symbol of that springtime she was forever trying to recapture.

He'd listened to her with half an ear, hardly at all. And no strong emotion in him over it—fuming with other headaches as he'd been then. *The big stuff*, the truer crises.

Good-by Again, he'd guessed Susan was saying all in all—the same fluttery speech Susan had made how many times before in their marriage?

A speech and pose that was flagrantly bad casting—a thirty-eight-year-old Juliet ridiculously trying to grow wings.

Before the sounds of the Harding station wagon had emptied into Laurel Hill Road, he'd been back in his study. On the long-distance phone to Brant, Bellows, Appleby and Harding. On Brant's own private line. Making with the ideas, pouring it on, goosing the old man into loverlike

16

responses—stealing a march on Bellows; cannily damning Stachel and Doobs with small praise for their job on that Pabst beer promotion. He'd remembered about Susan late that night. He'd come off the commuter's train, to find himself alone with Ingabord, the housekeeper.

He hadn't missed Susan at all that first night, or the next, or the next fifty. He'd, in fact, relished the freedom, like a man let out of jail after long imprisonment. Fun to the limit, and no shoddy lies, no morning-after guilts about it.

He'd begun to miss Susan only lately. The fun had begun to pall; he'd begun to feel lonely in the midst of gaiety.

Ingabord had quit; there were empty beer cans and whiskey bottles on window sills like targets in a shooting gallery, the lawn grass stood high as summer corn, he was buying new shirts and socks for the soiled dozens moldering in the laundry bag.

He'd of a sudden looked hard and sensibly at his life, and found it disorderly.

He hated disorder—he took morale from starched linen, gleaming candelabra, spit and polish, pin-neat surfaces.

And so, as in those other bust-ups, he was clear again about Susan's role in his scheme. She was a vital link in his chain of order—the alternative to Susan was demoralization.

And she was flesh of his young middle age, he now told himself with wry sentimentality. The scar tissue faded and so blended with the skin that the one thousand wounds of their fifteen connubial years were at least hidden, if not altogether healed.

Come hell or high water, he had to get her back. The

17

sense and logic of his life demanded it. He sorely needed her as an ally in his death struggle against Bellows, Appleby, Stachel and Doobs.

Harding lit a cigarette and shut off his thinking. He blew a smoke ring, then devised another, more perfect one. He fussed with his clothes, carefully adjusted the fall of his trousers, ran pinching fingers along them to restore the crease, seeking distractions so he could get out of the bog of himself.

The road signs now said *bajada,* and *despacio,* in a caution for slow speed on the steep hill ahead. Rufino recklessly disobeyed the signs, with one eye cocked to enjoy his passenger's agitation.

Harding tensed up, his thigh and leg muscles aching, one foot hard on the flat of the floorboard, as if braking the vehicle. He sensed the provocation as some test of his mettle; kid stuff, but also a nerve warfare with the *yanqui* —Rufino seeding vignettes he would later tell with impudent laughter at the expense of the moneyed *turistas.*

Harding steeled himself against any cry or protest over Rufino's wheelsmanship. He tried to concentrate on the music, relax with it, be relaxed by it. He turned the volume higher, but just as the *mariache* reached a crescendo and stopped. When a Spanish-language newscast commenced, he turned the Off knob.

Harding said brusquely, "How many kilometers now to Choluca?"

"*Nueve,* Señor—nine. We will soon make the turn into the Choluca road." Rufino admonished himself aloud, "I must watch for the sign with the arrow that says Choluca. And then I must look for the four graves." He looked full

18

at Harding, his eyes inviting a question about the legend of the four graves. When he read Harding's disinterest, he shrugged, muttering epithets under his breath.

Choluca lay tucked away from the tourist circuit proper. A narrow side road forming a straggly V with the highway cut into the heart of the village. The mouth of the road lay negligently in the brush, lower than the highway; a sudden drop with no gradation. It was part paved, part dirt, with the tracks of wagon wheels and animal hooves limned in the hard clay. It had rises and sudden gasping drops, like a roller coaster, as it twisted past cobblestoned yards, with stalls for burros and horses, bottoms visible and sometimes a head, and men under palm-leaf hats dozing on spread *petates*. There were houses: earth-brown adobes reflecting the sunshine goldenly, with dirt front courts dotted with conical ovens; and then the sturdier one-story houses with tiled roofs projecting like visors for shade.

Rufino waved at a group of chattering women around an ancient wall. "This is not yet Choluca," he said. "This is on the way to Choluca."

They passed one market, glimpsing displays of pottery, copper vessels, textiles, folk art, fruit, vegetables, and regionally costumed women with narrow sashes at the waist. On a height stood an ancient church, in an atrium of olive, ash and cedar trees. On its tower was a large stone hieroglyph of an ant. There were natives idling about the court, out of the sun, careless in serapes, careless of the day.

At one stage of the bruising ride, there was the echoing of gunshot. Rufino said, "They are shooting ducks to roast for the big ceremony—*Ofrendas* for the dead. Today is

El Día de los Muertos, the Day of the Feast of the Dead."

It piqued Harding's curiosity, but he feigned disinterest. Besides, speech on the gutted road was at the risk of tongue and teeth.

Rufino said critically, "It is not so clever to *shoot* the ducks. It is more clever to kill them with spears." He freed one hand to show the pantomime of harpooning, and simulated the cries of frightened ducks.

Harding said wrathfully, "Damn it to hell, drive with both hands!" He put fingers tenderly to his skull, where he'd struck it against a side pane of glass.

Rufino said cheerfully, "One more hill, and then perhaps one other one, and then the four graves, and we are surely in Choluca."

2

The highland slopes around Choluca were giant chessboards, with colored squares of corn, beans, squash, chili, sugar cane, tropical fruits, and abandoned clearings where a too-repetitious crop had soured the soil. The abundant harvest filled the market stands with surpluses that rotted to seed, or were exported to neighboring villages on primitive carts, in vintage Fords and Chevrolets, on the strong backs of pack animals, on human backs, the cargo secured by means of a strap on the forehead.

The village lay like a vast crater below the highlands; overbuilt in its center, and then sprawling along the edges of the slopes, scattered and at odd angles, as if blown from the hub by a gale. It looked dusty and windswept, despite the lush vegetation; the streams that were a circling figure eight had a top film of fine dust. The natives looked hot in their clothes; their mouths hung open and their lower lips were chronically drooping, as if in a sign of a perpetually unslaked thirst.

On a small wooden footbridge, a fellow in a wide hat pulled down to his nose sat cross-legged, casting a fisherman's net. The fish were surfaced, easily victim and no effort to it, stunned as they were by the powdered narcotic, barbasco, that coated the water.

Rufino guided the Cadillac in a slow crawl through Avenida Juárez, the village's main street. From time to time he tooted the car horn loudly, not so much as a precaution, but to grandly call attention to himself, his status behind the wheel of a fine, expensive limousine. The embarrassed Harding bore the gantlet of pedestrian stares, mentally vowing later reprisals against the chauffeur. A beggarly tip, *if* a tip at all; and he'd file a sharp complaint with that damned rental agency in Mexico City.

The Main Street look of Choluca was familiarly like a thousand others, as if the design of all of them had been copied from one master postcard. Long barracks-like blockhouses of cheap mortar; the façades uneven and crackled like the clay pottery around. Color-tone posters, with a pebbled effect from the stucco, lightened the monotony and momentarily won the eye. These scenes showed *toreros* in ballet stances and maddened bulls, a Mexican-produced film with Dolores Del Rio, a Hollywood-produced film with John Wayne looking hard-faced in an aviator's leather cap. The houses commonly had narrow outside porches like slum fire escapes. Galvanized tanks on the roofs provided "running water." Windows were enormous, as if the planning architect's sadistic intent were to bake the dwellers in the midday glare and heat, and freeze them in the midnight cold. There were fine houses, and finer haciendas, these remote from the center, some hewn into the hillside, with ornate façades, beautiful grounds and private roads.

There was a lively market, richly stocked and peculiarly carnival. Flowers in exotic rainbow variety; fruits with gay skins, and plump-bellied flies with metallic-toned wings. There were sellers of bread, large baked corn wafers, shrimps and dried fish, tamales, live and cooked iguanas, herbs, textiles, wickerware, *xicalpextles*. One *puesto* displayed diminutive things: miniatures of bone and ivory, metal and stone, tiny pictures made of colored straws, little flowers and small animals. The *mestizo* tending the stall was skillfully carving the kernel of a peach.

Today one wall of the market was arranged singularly as a bazaar of death. It was that November Festival of the Children and Adult Dead, the annual All Saints and Souls Days, when the village folk of all ages trooped after dark to gaily decorated cemeteries, to holiday and make festive with the dead.

These *puestos*, bedecked with flaring orange marigolds, showed specially prepared foods and fruits, candies and breads shaped into imitation skulls, crossbones and skeletons—delights to be eaten graveside, by moonlight and burning tapers. In some booths there were wares of clay toys, symbols and mementos, some remarkably inventive, and accenting the childlike ease of Latinized people before their saints and their dead. There was a gaily jiggling gilt skeleton across one booth, and a queue of laughing and enchanted children busily licking-biting candy tombstones made of almond paste. There were toy coffins made up of gumdrops, and bright-colored hearses of a size a two-year-old could trundle behind him.

One Indian, eyeless more than merely blind, with the sockets empty, sat on the ground with a display of his art-craftsmanship at his feet. *Veinte centavos*—a neatly lettered card announced the cost. Harding looked with fascination at what he had cleverly devised: an animated pasteboard view of the vanity of life, wherein priest, peon, soldier, worker, statesman, bullfighter, wife, wench, arise out of darkness, cross a tiny stage, and descend into darkness on the other side.

An end booth was an exhibit purely, with no goods offered for sale. This held a scale-model cemetery, with the more imposing tombs fitted as chapels, graves fluttering with paper streamers, the tombstones jolly in pink and blue trimmings.

Choluca was a village of bizarre contrasts: there were two worlds simultaneously, one culture cocooned in the other. A primitivism, old as it was, endured, with those things that were new in machinery, styles, and even custom fed into the ancient stocks, and even lost among them. Agriculture was hardly more than one step forward from the digging stick; crude plows and hoes outnumbered and dwarfed the few tractors and gasoline-fed machines. Liquor was distilled in primitive stills; a silver craftsman used modern stamps and dies. On an unmarked street a short stroll from the hub, a *mestizo* at an ancient forge was shoeing a burro; some doors away, an Indian in faded blue fatigues was soaking the carburetor of a panel delivery truck in a basin of kerosene.

There were doctors with stocks of antibiotics; a witch doctor could also be found with a magic remedy for blue spots on the skin. These were predominantly Catholic people, yet they voodooistically sprinkled the ground with the blood of turkeys and chickens, to render it fertile, and to hex their enemies and make the boundary inviolable.

Close by the Choluca market, an ancient church stood like a stone image in the mirror of Time. There were contradictory stories about the site of the Church San Felipe: it stood on the site that had once been an ancient slave market; another version had it that it had been built over the ruins of an earlier church, in keeping with Cortez's oath to replace every pagan temple with a church of Christ.

The façade of the church was covered with tiles, a great many of them broken and scorched by the attrition of time and weather. The porch and cupolas were upheld by round tile columns of unique design. The patio was a cloistered yard lying between the priest's quarters and the church, shaded by aged and withering poinsettia and bougainvillaea trees and vines. A tile-balustraded stairway led up to the belfry; a great iron bell hung tonguelessly, with wide cracks all over its cone. A rabble of Mexicans, boys and men, lounged in the shaded yard—proof, of sorts, of the much-bandied saying that the church in Mexico was mainly the poor man's palace. The loungers nibbled at food, sipped drinks, pitched pennies, quarreled among themselves when the ennui became too burdensome.

Rufino parked the limousine in a square directly across from the Church San Felipe. The parking square was filled, curiously enough, with custom Jaguars, M.G.'s, Renaults, Chryslers, Cadillacs. An index, this, of the invasion of Choluca by visitors and in-residence expatriates, the *norteamericanos* and the Europeans.

Rufino groaned out of his seat. On the curb, he pointed to an inn neighboring the church. "I will ask there in the Choluca Hotel. And after that, in the Casa Cámara."

Harding asked frowningly, "Where is the Casa Cámara?"

Rufino pointed in a direction. "Three, four streets, Señor Harding."

"Inquire in the Choluca Hotel," Harding said. "If my wife isn't there, report back and drive me to the Casa Cámara." A look of irritation crossed his face. "Don't leave me hung up in a parking lot."

Rufino smiled broadly. "I will be back in *un momento*." He went off slowly, as if at once absent-minded about his destination and errand.

Harding lit a cigarette then crushed it. He was nervous again, itching as if a colony of ants were bivouacking on his hide. He stared bleakly out of the car window, and then, to break the oppressive feeling of confinement, he got out of the car. He crossed the street to the church, forcing interest in the sights around him. He peered into the shaded yard, forming mechanical impressions, then he entered the building.

Inside the church, Indians clad in blue fatigues and shoed in *huaraches* were working long bamboo poles with feathers on the end, dusting saints, shrines, the rococo and intricately decorated high altar. They did this listlessly, in the somnambulism of unsupervised household servants saving themselves. When one of them passed the altar, he genuflected reverently, as if he knew that *this* expenditure was beheld and evaluated by watching eyes.

A great corner shrine of the Healing Virgin, standing with open arms and ornamented with much gold leaf, had a collection of relics before her, piled oddly like a bonfire waiting for the match, these relics—crutches, braces, bandages, casts, crude drawings of accidents, shootings, stabbings, near-murder—all offered as proof of that imminent death that had been averted by fortunate and saintly intercession.

Before this shrine, a man in beggar's clothes with hardly a face stayed on his knees in whispering devotions. There was a scattering of *centavos* on the floor beside him, either fallen from his pockets or offered as the cost for that favor he sorely wanted.

Of the numerous miraculous Christ figures in niches and spaced around the walls, one dead corpus on the Cross was painted black—the handiwork of some prankster, violator or dissenter. The black was roughly laid on the original baked enamel, the uniformity now of black color for the whole figure and face voiding that theme of the cruel crown of thorns, the agonized face, the blood running vividly from gashes and wounds.

The priest in charge was Father Porfirio, a man of essentially Franciscan simplicity, with little of the spiritual psychomancy and expansiveness of so many of his priestly fellows. Father Porfirio abided the panoply of his church, either shunned the grandees, politicians, chauvinists and bigots or roasted them on the prongs of his sardonic humor. He dressed plainly, approving of the law which dictated the wearing of the maniple rather than the cassock; he busied himself less with the Doctrine and more with the ordinary chores of baptism, marriage, confession, administering the Sacrament, giving extreme unction and burials. He was popular with the Spanish-Mexicans, just a whit less popular with the Indians—failing these latter as he did in their childlike and pagan imagination, their penchant for idolatry.

The sermon he'd preached earlier this day had been keyed to the admonition of the Apostle Paul, in the book of Romans, "Every one of us shall give account of himself to God." For the conclusion of his sermon, Father Porfirio had quoted from memory from Proverbs XV:3: " 'The eyes of the Lord are in every place, beholding the evil and the good.' "

3

Rufino stood somnambulistically in the shade of the coconut palms in the front plaza of Choluca's Casa Cámara. He wore a frayed white cotton suit and held a shabby straw hat in one hand. Sweat ran down his cheeks to his clothes, as if fed by secret springs in his skull. Bubbles of water hung delicately and ornamentally from his nostrils and the lobe of one ear. The low hang of his trousers distorted his form, made him look top-heavy and freakish. When he saw Harding beckon impatiently to him, he resumed his snail's walk back to the car.

The chauffeur said with glistening eyes, "*Sí*, this is where the Señora Harding is staying. Only she is not here now."

He proudly thumbed his coat lapel to show a miniature dancing skeleton attached to the buttonhole. "I am given this in the Casa Cámara." He heaved his frame so the skeleton jiggled grotesquely. "Is funny, ha, Mr. Harding?" Rufino laughed goldenly.

"What weird—" Harding frowned disapprovingly.

"To celebrate *los muertos*." Rufino reached into a pocket, then offered a confection to Harding, a gumdrop candy shaped like a miniature skull.

Harding shook his head to the offering. "Too damned morbid for my tastes," he said, uncomfortably aware that he was playing Rufino's game.

"We are friendly to our dead." Rufino looked archly at Harding, then bit vigorously into the candy.

"You're a bunch of idiots," Harding said. "Did they say where Mrs. Harding might have gone?"

"*Sí*," Rufino said in his rhythmic speech. "If she is not in the Galería Tajín, then you are to look for her in the Villa de la Soledad." A hand motioned limply in the direction of the highland slopes, and there was a drop of tone. "*Ya revienta de madura*—high, high up there, see? The Señora has good friends in the villa."

Harding stared at the chauffeur's flaming cheeks. "You're drunk," he said. "You slopped up a few in the Choluca Hotel, and now again in Casa Cámara."

Rufino cast his eyes down slyly. "For the thirst," he said. "I drink for the thirst, and not the tequila." He faced his patron boldly now. "You are surely not thinking to drive back to Mexico City today?"

"Not with you at the wheel, that's for sure." Harding slammed out of the car. "How do I find this Galería Tajín?"

Rufino pointed up the street. "Walk straight this way and you will find it." His mouth turned down at the corners. "You are not going without Rufino?"

Harding thrust money at the chauffeur. "Get a room and sleep off the tequila," he said. "I'll be back for you." He walked a few steps, then came back to take the car keys out of the ignition.

Harding jingled the car keys before Rufino. "I'll hold on to these," he said with a wink that brought a wide grin to Rufino's face.

4

The music pouring through a loud speaker could be heard out in the street. The jazz recordings "Who's Afraid of Love" and "S'posin'" played back to back, with Fats

Waller on the piano and vocalizing his spoof of the sentimental songs, backed by the rhythms of a guitarist and a
drummer.

The *Galería Tajín* was one of some six cellar lounges
where expatriates gathered to loaf, listen to music, talk
literature, art, politics, over drinks of tequila—tequila drunk
with *punctilio*, with the cut of lemon and with salt on
the back of the hand.

The jazzophiles and intellectuals looked odd with their
sprays of chin whiskers, and dressed in corduroy jackets
and rumpled slacks, or were conspicuously stylish in the
summer modes of the metropolitan cities and spas of the
north.

These men and women, the young ones and the older
ones, the rich ones and the poor ones, colonized within
Choluca, forming an aristocracy of sorts. They lived co-
hesively within their own colony, perhaps aware intuitively that these two cultures could only meet and never
blend. Their chief point of contact with Cholucans, other
than perfunctory pleasantries, was in the shops and markets,
in those available service trades. The richer expatriates
lived splendidly in well-staffed houses, and were, for this,
important hirers of domestic labor. The money, of course,
was welcome in Choluca; and if only for this, the expatriate horde was tolerated. What dislike, or worse,
Cholucans deeply felt for these poseurs and patrons was
only subtly communicated.

What made Choluca popular with expatriates, over
Mexico City, Acapulco, Rome, Paris, Capri, could not be
stated exactly. Choluca had been mysteriously selected,
and the greater mystery was that this popularity grew
steadily. What *could* be stated exactly was the general and

individual reason for expatriation. There were bohemians, searchers for Xanadu, political exiles, refugees, disenfranchised intellectuals. They wrote poetry, novels, plays, political tracts, composed music, sculpted, painted, annotated Freud, defended Wilhelm Reich and Henry Miller. Most lived on inheritances and accumulated wealth, some on hoarded savings and pensions, some on manuscript and art sales to markets in New York, Chicago, California, others as parasites, moochers, lovers, guests. A few were in business in Mexico: in real estate, copper and silver crafts, travel, poultry, whatever Mexican law allowed, or could be bribed or otherwise induced to overlook.

There were come-lately expatriates in Choluca, and some others who could count their stay in years.

Harding descended the short flight of steps tentatively, a little afraid of braving the deafening din below.

The stone walls of the cellar *galería* were calcimined white; high-wattage spotlights painted silver were beamed on the hung oils, gouaches, water colors. The ceiling was low and covered with a fabric of dusty brown netting; thick smoke vapors from pipes and cigarettes stayed statically at eye level and made bodies in certain areas of the cellar look headless.

Harding first oriented his eyes, then threaded carefully through the pack. He saw two women successively who he imagined were Susan, and both times had to disengage himself from arch and spontaneous friendship. He stopped to stare closely at one immense painting, a pointillism of large dots like mice droppings, only the dots and no other detail. To further confound the eye, there were the spattered carcasses of insects plunked against the flats of whitewashed brick on both sides of the painting. He stooped over to read the title of the painting. Composition Number 5, it said meaninglessly. The signature on the painting was as un-Mexican as the cellar: Diana Osgood.

The honeycomb mesh oozed new music into the cellar now. "Sweetie Pie," with Milton Mezzrow's soft clarinet and Floyd O'Brien's whispering trombone.

Harding roamed the cellar now in a reconnaissance around the walls, with staring stops before hazy galaxies, to resolve or dissolve Susan. He completed the oblong of room fruitlessly, and stood gaping once more before another hanging oddity, a white canvas overpainted white, in its center, and raising out, a small plastic box used by fishermen to store fishhooks. He made out the contents of the plastic box; there were dried curls of paint squeezed right from the tube, and a green-glass emerald like an eye set into the gook.

He heard voices behind him discussing the painting: a male voice high up in the nose, and a female voice unnaturally gruff, as if with laryngitis. The talk was unintelligible to his ears, over his head—he understood just a few words of it, much like a foreigner grasping at a strange tongue.

As with the other vaulting, brain-busting talk he'd overheard while moving around the cellar. American voices, mainly, and some of them well-bred tones, but using idea patterns and value-jammed phrases he could only feed into his mind in bites and bits, and with extraordinary concentration.

He shrugged it away, washed his mind of it. All garbage lost in the backwash of the old dormitory days—how many years ago had it been?

He paused at the exit for a last look at the cellar and its denizens. *Scum*—Harding reached a sweeping verdict. Half-assed painters, dilettantes, Jaguar intellectuals, queers and commies. He nodded wisely with the last. *Commies*—he'd understood just enough of the jabber to be able to finger a half-dozen of them in the *galería*. And good riddance, was his final thought about it now. Mexico was welcome to the lot of them.

A new recording followed his ascent of the cellar stairs to the street. "Sweet Sue"—Harding found himself setting his feet down to it, whistling to it. It had been the song of his courtship of Susan, marvelously in theme because of the coincidence of names.

5

It was Sunday open house, as a hundred Sundays before, at the Villa de la Soledad. The hostess of *the* ranking salon in the expatriate colony was Lisa Franke, half-American, half-European, still provocatively in her middle years.

The Villa de la Soledad nuzzled into an almost vertical slope; it had an impressive blue-and-white-tile façade, a sculptured gray stone doorway and niches. Walks on three sides of it were shaded by old *ahuehuete* trees, pines, eucalyptus. Its foreground was a plaza with an old fountain centered, and perched on it the figure of a frog playing a mandolin. There were separate terraces built on two levels; from the topmost one it was as if the languid semi-tropical village below lay in a picturesque ravine.

The house was nearly two centuries old, inevitably a museum one day soon in a country jealous of its treasure. It had thirty-four rooms; the interior walls were covered with colored mosaics, murals of fiestas with *conchero* dancers performing, oils that joined centuries as if all time were a mere shift of the eye, with works by Cabrera and Villalpando, and also Orozco and Rivera. There were priceless frescoes reproducing pre-Conquest scenes, painted around the walls of four vestibules.

On the highest terrace, the old man named Max Marsant sat still as a statue. He was alone, lonely in himself, as the sick and aged are. He was in an electrically powered wheel chair, complete with driving gears, simple to operate without a nurse or any attendant. He sat tall in his chair, his eyes slitted in half-sleep and his chin lumped up to his nose as if he'd swallowed his lips. He was seventy, in some stage of Parkinson's disease, more dead than alive; a nuisance to the living, brushed impatiently into odd corners—as if full sight of Max revolted the eye, like a foreshadowing of one's own decay.

The four-o'clock sun was behind him, beaming over a shoulder like an electric bulb located to give maximum light to the canvas on the easel. He had paint brushes tied to both arms, up to the crook of the elbow. The ties were strong leather thongs bound around his naked arms so that the brush bristles extended so-much beyond his fingertips.

The subject on the canvas was foreign to any of the village scenes below. It was something posed by memory and the senses only: a tilted flat of earth set starkly in limbo, a café table built of cabbage roses, and nudes seated in a semicircle with their genitalia exposed to the viewer. All of the figures were male: one a frail boy in first puberty, and the last one an overfleshed voluptuary with pocked skin. Features were indistinct, as if in the mists, or as if the decomposed look here was intentional with the artist. The canvas looked as if it had been carefully constructed and detailed, and then left to time and the weather to blur and dechemicalize so that it would look as it did now.

The old man's hand moved slowly; the brush found the canvas at its bottom edge, then moved wormlike up to where Max wanted to put the paint.

6

The ground-level salon was enormous, unnerving to anyone sensitive to space. There were no walls on two sides of it, where this room joined with two other rooms, with hardly a threshold marking any boundary. The furniture stood unusually high, on legs like stilts, in a decorative trick to lower the sky of a ceiling. There were thick layers of rugs, as if the first plan were storage; the walking sensation was like being on thick grass after a deluging rain.

Great chandeliers with tiers of glinting crystals hung awesomely like threatening weights. They held the eye hypnotically; guests made nervous by them crossed the rooms in routes that avoided the center.

Those guests already present looked stunted, a race of dwarfs, like wood and glass miniatures toppled to the cushiony rugs from high shelves. They loitered in pairs and cliques in the three rooms. They were lethargic in their fun, talked in low, confidential tones, mouth to ear. They held their drinking glasses like raised torches, in mutual rituals of toasting, drank tastelessly and desperately as if the blood was becalmed and the alcohol was the saving ingredient.

The hi-fi was playing, with the volume muted to contain the music to one area. The piece was very modern: George Shearing's "Black Satin."

A stubby, glossily bald fellow sat close to the speaker box. There was a small, battered valise on the floor, secured between his legs; a hand kept feeling for it absently and regularly, over and over, as if its owner was anxious for its safety. The man's eyes were bland, agate-dead, as if this were one set imposed on his active own that lay hidden underneath. His jowls hung limply, gnarled and dry of juice like old leather, and so low he showed no neck. He seemed self-absorbed, uninterested in the salon and the people, with a sub-charge of hostility that might erupt with the merest provocation of trespass, small talk, any attempted camaraderie. He had his head turned sharply toward the speaker box, his eyes slitted and his brow intense, as if trying vainly to decipher some strange, atonal tongue.

As the music beat against him, but eluding him, his pantomime became bizarre. His face reddened and swelled; blood filled veins in his eyes.

Modern music, he railed silently in his mind, sweeping Shearing into that catchall sack of exhibits of bourgeois decadence and degeneracy.

He now flipped the pages of those books of personal story and history woven as one that he would write tomorrow soon; seeking to wrest from limbo an experience he could associate to this one now with Shearing. He soon found the page, smiling with the holiday of ego it refurbished for him.

A Shostakovich opera was being performed in a Moscow theater—1939—he hazarded the year. The libretto was based on the then Russian classic by Leskov, titled *The Lady Macbeth of the Mzensk District,* in which a woman murders her husband and then her lover and herself. He had attended the opera, along with other Party elite, sitting but four seats removed from Stalin and Molotov. Sensitive to Stalin's black disapproval, he had personally, two years later, led the outcry against the opera, denouncing it for its modernism and bourgeois decadence.

A new record played now. An alley-den, barrel-house-blues number, "Steamboat Romp," with orchestrated whistle blasts shrieking through the polyphony that splintered the ears.

He turned away from the speaker box, sealed himself in deafness, and holidayed through other pages and chapters of those books he must write tomorrow soon, in exile here in Mexico. *Must write*—he vowed the words savagely, fighting down waves of sickness that were lately a chronic complement to any review of his yesterdays. New pages written and submitted to posterity for those older pages of textbooks, histories, news files, now being rewritten by party puppets and historians, with his name and deeds erased.

7

In a second salon, remote from the music, a handsome two-toned-wood television set stood incongruously beside a lighted glass case with a valuable collection of small jaguar gods in colored jadeite. The television set was on; a Mexican-produced motion picture was in its final reel. An old Cantinflas starrer, with the ingénue enacted by Donna Flores, a dark beauty with a high-bridged nose, large, almond-shaped, slanting eyes, a small, full mouth with sensuous arched lips.

The movie had a Spanish-language dialogue track; the ingénue spoke fluently, at home with the tongue, with only slight traces of the glottal stop, the liquid singsong of the Zapotec Indian.

The sitting couple were absorbed in the film. Their hands showed matching wedding bands: heavy yellow gold, wide almost to the knuckle of the hand. The woman wore a loose tunic that bellied out in front as if a wind had stolen under her skirt. She was pregnant, in the end months of it; she breathed in sucking gasps, pumping her bosom high with each intake of air.

The man was of medium height, swart-complexioned, with a running scar that showed white like a streak of paint beginning on the neck and continuing halfway up the cheek. There were scribbles of gray in the luxuriantly black and vaselined crop of hair—premature, this, since he was hardly more than thirty. His eyes were the color of coal, with the oily sheen of black olives.

He watched the film with eyes wetter than usual, as if in his secret thoughts trysting with the glamorous Donna Flores. The woman with him watched the film more critically, with that quiet of a female eyeing a rival, methodically entering those debits and credits in Vanity's ledger, of comparative anatomy, face, make-up, hair-do, personality.

The woman said judgingly, "Much too skinny, and the hair-do is bad for the face. See, Vito? The brow is small and round. With the hair falling on it, she looks like a beetle!"

Vito said jokingly, "If beetles looked like that, I'd stock myself a harem." He patted her hand. "You're at least twice as beautiful nowadays, Donna."

Donna clumped fingers in her belly. "I'm at least twice as fat!"

"Hey, I've forgotten the compliment." Vito frowned. "What's that Indian word again?"

"Frondosa"—Donna laughed with big, white teeth— "only it is Zapotec, not merely Indian."

"Frondosa, and how!" A hand possessively traced her bottom and flanks. "Zapotecs and Italians see eye to eye on that much. We like our women to be plump."

Donna laughed. *"Frondosa* means literally a great, leafy tree. To the Zapotec, slim women are rachitic; thinness is a sign of bad health." She stared at the screen now, and her brow ridged reminiscently. "It was only my second movie—and acting with Cantinflas! I could not sleep nights; on the set I would keep forgetting my lines. Poor Ruiz was driven mad—he would never again direct me in a picture, he swore."

Vito's face darkened. "Let Ruiz fry in hell. He's a conceited louse—he can't decide whether he's De Mille or De Sica!"

Donna said, "Ruiz was assistant to Sergei Eisenstein, when Eisenstein came to Mexico. Eisenstein is still his God—Ruiz has a film library of Eisenstein pictures that he runs off and studies."

Vito was glaring angrily, as if somewhere in her remarks he sensed a last-ditch loyalty to Ruiz, a slighting of him.

Donna smiled now, kissed his cheek, and got off the subject. Ruiz had been her husband before Vito Avedon. Now as a daily goad to Vito's jealousies, there was six-year-old Domingo, the son in her custody sired by Ruiz. Domingo was uncannily the image of his father; a Trojan horse in Vito's psyche and in his house.

Vito switched channels before the picture credits. He looked around the room restlessly. "Where are the rest of the people?"

"There is an art exhibit in the village today," Donna said.

"At the Galería Tajín, from four to seven. I received a circular in the mail." She laughed lightly. "Lisa's open house is only the *second* attraction in Choluca today."

Vito made no answer, and Donna said, "It is two artists in a combined show. That young American who wears the pie on his head." She touched far down her cheek, then cupped a hand under her chin. "And the hair here, and there."

"Who is the other artist?" Vito made conversation.

"The Canadian girl, the one from Montreal."

"Oh." He smirked knowingly. "The les on the motor scooter."

"Vito, that is mean!"

"A man can't tell a les from a woman!" Vito laughed broadly.

"You flirted with her," Donna said, smiling. "She didn't flirt back. So you condemn her."

"Enough with the les." Vito winked at his wife. "I don't want you too sophisticated, too smart. You might forget what comes naturally, start tricking it up."

Donna said in mock complaint, "Yet you are always disillusioning me in people—always teaching me horrible things."

"It's an automatic thing with me," Vito answered seriously. "What's the vice, what's the twist? I meet anybody, that's my first thought. What aren't they showing, what's behind the nice manners?" His face shadowed and the running scar raised and reddened now as if newly welted. "I saw some pretty raw stuff back in the States—I knew as much at ten as I know now. The dirt and dirty stuff, I mean."

Donna looked intently at her husband. There were

flutterings in her chest now, a suddenly more rapid heartbeat. *Not* from her condition—she was clinical about her symptoms. It was the recurring dread, old as this marriage: her qualms about Vito. She knew him only in his habit with her. Beyond that, bulking in mystery, was his longer time before her. And that life unrevealed to her, except symptomatically—Vito's thrashing sleep, the night cries, his dark skin rubbed with the chalk of shock, the swift asthmatic attacks and then the desperate emergency of the steam tent, the holy crucifix ever present as if glued to his palm.

Donna blurted out, as if the thoughts haunting her mind formed their own speech, "Vito, don't you ever get homesick?" She'd asked it endlessly.

She knew his unfailing reaction to the questions; she could accurately describe it even with her back turned and her eyes off him. There would first be pain, a clear sign of it. Then her husband would slip a hand into his pocket, keep it there clutching the crucifix until the tensions in his hand made veins bulge through the skin of his temples. Then finally a stiff actorish pose, a feigned lightness of retort, stilted, false, unnaturally voiced.

Vito said, "Sure I get homesick. What's with the old bunch, I wonder. Who's grown old, fat, who's still poor, who's dead? And did they finally get that park-playground on Maujer and Van Dyck?" He laughed synthetically. "I was nineteen-about when I left Detroit—the park was already ten years overdue then."

Donna said, "Vito, talk about your people!"

His eyes on her were sightless now, his mouth turned up in the mechanical figure of a smile. "At thirty-one, who thinks of his family?"

His eyes closed momentarily, and Donna saw the tell-tale veins raise burstingly on the sides of his temples. *He's praying*, she thought; *silently in his mind*. Clutching the crucifix in his pocket and begging forgiveness of God.

Vito's gesture caught her unawares. He patted her stomach; a hard, bouncing pat, then smaller ones until his hand lay flat and hard on her. "My family's in here," he said.

She put a hand over his, to blanket the chill she felt inside. "But you have a mother and father, and two sisters and a brother. You have been here in Mexico for twelve, thirteen years. Vito, you *must* be lonesome for them!"

She knew his next speech before he made it. He spoke it by rote, as if reading from a script in his mind, every time the question was put to him.

"The times I get lonesome, I just dream them up—simple?" His stare fixed distantly. "Mama's in the kitchen, fat as a sausage, her dress six inches at least above her slip. My father's in his wheel chair reading *Il Corriere Italiano*, and out of the side of his eye casing the action in the street from the window. He fell three stories once on a roofing job and cracked his spine, the poor bastard." He added parenthetically, "We live in a one-family frame house; my father grows figs in the back yard.

"The kids are doing the usual. Josie's with her school homework; Grace is sneaking lipstick on in the john—she's twelve, with a shape like twenty. Tommy's down in the cellar with some other kid, smoking cigarette butts, trying to inhale without coughing up his guts." Vito smiled bleakly. "Tommy's seven, with a blond mop of hair—like some Swede got to Mama."

Donna tried to keep from screaming it: "But you remember them as they were *twelve years ago!*"

"What's bad about that?" His eyes fixed peculiarly on Donna. "They don't age a day in twelve years. I think that's pretty good."

She said now, as so many times before, "It would be nice for your parents to visit here. I want so much to know them."

When he nodded mechanically as she'd expected, Donna said, "Or *we* should visit Detroit. That way I can know your whole family."

"They're nice people," he said woodenly. "Mama's always forcing food on you—you'll have to get used to that. My father doesn't talk—say hello to him, and he's deaf." His eyes closed tightly, there was a wriggling of cloth where his coat pocket was, and the veins in his temples knobbed out.

"Watch your smokes around Tommy—the little bugger will sure as hell steal your pack. Hide your handbag under a sofa pillow or somewhere, so Grace can't cop your lipstick." He frowned slightly. "Who's left? Yeah, Josie. Josie's a brain—get talking to her, and you're dead. She'll show off everything she's ever learned."

Vito got up on his feet. He stood trancelike, on weak legs as if about to keel over in a faint. Then his eyes opened abnormally round, dispelling visions, seeking back to the reality of time and the salon.

"Excuse me while I go get a drink." The voice was now more familiarly her husband's. He arched questioning brows at her, and Donna pointed a finger at her stomach.

"Oh, I forgot." Vito grinned weakly. "You drink, and *two* of you get loaded."

He stared at her, in possession of himself now. "You keep asking me the same questions. How many years are we married?"

"Three," Donna said tremulously.

"Two stock questions I missed." Vito tried to make his tone a bantering one. "What brought me to Mexico in the first place, and why am I here so long." He smiled. "Want to answer them for yourself?"

Donna said tonelessly, "You love Mexico."

"It's the land of milk and honey." His tone was buoyant. "I came here wet behind the ears, without a button, and *now* look at me! I'm big in real estate, I'm married to glamor." He kissed fingers to her stomach. "And I'm going to rack up five kids."

"Why do you always say the number *five?*" There was a wild quality in Donna's voice.

He recoiled again, in that way she knew so well. Her eyes followed his hand to a pocket, and then her look transferred to his eyes and temples.

"Five"—Vito had trouble steadying his underlip—"I owe God five lives."

8

With Vito gone off to get his drink, Donna gave herself to her secret and unspoken surmise about her husband. The excessive emotion of his faith, his look to God only with eyes of fear—Vito was a murderer haunted by his victims, was her verdict. An uncaught murderer, caught awfully now in the toils of his own conscience. *Five lives*—she shuddered over his phrase, what it revealed. Her mind filled with movies and scenes from movies, exported from the United States to Mexico, that she had seen over the years. Men resembling Vito, Italian faces and a silken look, cruel-eyed executioners in black suits firing submachine-gun bursts into cafés, garages, sidewalk throngs, and then, later, at bay and dying terribly in the crumbling fortress that was a tenement building or a rural hide-out.

Two scenes of climax were particularly remembered, for frightfulness, and for that inevitability of retribution that proved her own deepest moral beliefs. She'd seen both movies on one bill, reissued and paired as classics of the gangster genre. One climax before her inner eye showed a dying killer, coughing and hemorrhaging blood, crawling up the high stone steps of a church. Her eye moved in close-up on the dying man's face, discerned it to be Vito's. The other climax showed a profile of Vito, unmistakable because of his running facial scar, face down in a city gutter, his blood mixing in with the river of rain water flowing downstreet to the sewer.

She shook her head, distraught for Vito, anguished for herself. Her eyes fixed on her high stomach, as if looking through to the fully formed and curling infant. She felt the kicks come now, saw the fabric of her clothes flutter with them.

She regretted this soon-born child, as she had Domingo in his time. She'd chosen the husband and father badly in Ruiz, and now even worse in Vito: Ruiz demanding virgins as if youth could be transfused through sex; and Vito sick and deeply disturbed, bargaining prayer and penitence for God's mercy.

She thought of her life and shook her head morosely. Her fame had been quick, then over after the shortest season, and now the long balance of her time lay hopelessly before her. There would be a third man after Vito, and then a fourth, and another and so on, in her search for that first mate she'd somehow missed in her most eligible hour. She hated Ruiz mainly for that—he'd cost her love. Disabled her for love, and perhaps forever.

In her mind now, she journeyed home—rode back to those fields of her girlhood. She placed herself on the same train that had brought her across the Isthmus from Ixtepec in Mexico South, and before that, by bus from her native Juchitán.

The rattling and overcrowded train, an assortment of boxcars and coaches, huffed and whined through jungles of giant trees hung with creepers, ragged palms, great taro leaves, and *plantanilla*. She saw again, as then, the chilling omen of black vultures sunning themselves on the topmost branches of bleached skeletons of great silk-cotton trees. She'd sat tensely on the coach seat beside Ruiz, a talent discovery and new bride both, riding north to the fabled world that was Mexico City. She'd had this sense of losing something irrecoverably, of yielding up more than could ever be returned to her. And in those moments when they passed the dead silk-cotton trees and the squatting vultures, cold chills had gone through her, as if her heart were a dripping block of ice. To her eye then, Ruiz's face was the awesome stranger-face it had been only nine weeks before when he'd arrived in Juchitán with actors, a technical crew, and equipment for location shooting of scenes of a movie.

He'd sat insensitive to her, in his own preoccupation, as if he'd already dismissed her from mind. As if she was just more company freight crated and stamped with his name, in transit from Juchitán to Mexico City.

She reversed the train stops, *Chinameca, Jáltipan, Ojapa, Almagres, Juile, Medias Aguas, Súchil*, yearning in her mind. Her eye reveled in the nearly forgotten, sorely missed sights and impressions—the milling food vendors in the stations hawking pieces of tough chicken, enchiladas, fruits, the primeval *Mixe* women proud in their yellow- and red-striped *huipiles* that showed off their amazingly pointed breasts, with white-toweled heads cushioning the baskets of fine pineapples. Leaving Matías Romero, the gate to Zapotec country, with the green-mantled look sharply changed now to the gray and rust of cereus cactus, as the jungle stopped before rolling hills, Donna felt her heaviness dissolve, as if she'd been systematically shedding those clothes, trappings, finery and weights she'd taken on from that first hour of her ride north and since. She felt free and unburdened once more, a marvelous nakedness, after so long—she could feel her skin, as if crustings had been burned away.

In *Ixtepec*, she scorned the bus that clattered Juchitán-ward. Instead she walked barefoot, with flowing nudity under the merest garments, over cobbled streets, and then over corrugated roads and dusty river beds, her eye on the sky melee of screeching green parrots.

Soon she ran, with scalding tears and in a fever of homesickness, as the first scattered houses of Juchitán began to appear—some of brick, most with walls made of woven branches plastered with mud and roofed with red tile. She ran desperately, with her heart pounding in bursts, threading the story in her mind, that awful story she would tell her people: her abduction through the device of marriage, into bondage, sophistication and sin. A panderer with a dwarf's head named Ruiz had come to Juchitán, to ship human cargo north to the elegant hotels and bagnios, after first sampling the fruit himself.

She saw Vito weaving drunkenly back across the salon. She prepared herself, so Vito would find her smiling.

9

The two men and the woman grouped before the small portable bar. The native behind the bar wore a white half-coat; he had solemn eyes and stood deafly, as if his ears were stopped.

The woman was Susan Harding, cream-skinned with a healthy glow, provocative in a tight skirt and wide leather belt with a uniquely tooled buckle, busty in a red blouse drawn very tightly into the belt. She had one foot sportively on the short brass rail. She drank with a certain bravado, as if perhaps an amateur at it.

The two men were of sharply contrasting types. The big-framed one, Alec Taylor, had close-cropped hair, a high brow that looked welted, an aquiline nose with a deep dent near the eye cradle. His eyes were in continual use, mobile but oddly unfocused, as if what he viewed was meaningless to him, like a blur of pedestrian faces on a public street. He wore a wide-knit polo shirt open at the throat, a tweed sport jacket and slacks. He looked like a miner from the Basque provinces in Spain. He was, how-ever, an American, a graduate of the University of Wis-consin. Occupation: screen writer.

The second man was of an age with Alec Taylor; both

were forty-four. This one was petite, as if boxed up in infancy to abort growth. He had small hands and feet, bunched features the span of a boy's hand, a wisping mustache black-penciled in those places where no hair had developed. He wore a blue sport shirt and rumpled seersucker trousers that hung low and caught in his heel. An imp look, all in all, except for the eyes. The eyes calculated advantages, ceaselessly sought the chink in your armor—they glittered in a rodent's head. He was Victor Hertzig, entrepreneur, a citizen of the world traveling on a Swiss passport.

Taylor poured himself a stiff hooker from a pinch-bottle, disdaining the bartender. He gestured the glass at Victor Hertzig and said offensively, "How many of these does it take to erase you?"

Hertzig smiled, and the mustache was temporarily submerged in the fold of his upper lip. "You're drinking yourself sober, Alec."

"Drinking himself into the grave!" Susan said anxiously. "Alec, if you must kill yourself, a bullet is quicker. Why prolong it?"

"It's better melodrama like this." Taylor winked at her. "The Great Man dissipates to a shadow of himself, tch, tch. Your way, we'd have no suspense. Or story enough for more than one reel."

Taylor downed his drink, splashing it against the wall of his throat without wetting his lips. He said, "As a kid, I used to watch my father drink like that. Head back, and down the hatch—one swallow and that's all. Mind you, uncut alcohol, and better than a hundred and fifty proof."

Hertzig said, "Their generation had iron constitutions."

Susan said, "Alec has ulcers—pretty bad, too."

Hertzig said, "Your Alec has *tsurus*." He saw Susan frown over the word and interpreted the Yiddicism. "The word means troubles."

Susan nodded glumly and reached a hand to pat Alec comfortingly. He drew away, then poured from the bottle once more. "I'm drinking purely as a connoisseur of fine old Scotch—you people have it wrong." He held up the bottle. "Read the label."

Susan said, "You'll hemorrhage again, you'll be getting emergency blood transfusions."

"Remind me never to confide in you again," Taylor said. He downed his drink in his hurried way. "Scotch like this is an elixir; forms a protective coating around your ulcer. What do doctors know!"

Hertzig spoke to Susan. "Let him celebrate—he's got the best reason to celebrate." His eyes shifted to watch Taylor's face slyly. "How often does a writer win the Academy Award for Best Screenplay?"

Taylor said blandly, "Victor's on a fishing expedition."

Hertzig said, "The identity of alias Lester Gates is about as secret as the measurements of Jayne Mansfield's bosom. Come, my genius friend, nobody is fooled." He nudged Taylor's ribs. "Go do the dramatic thing. The one perfect retort to the blacklist and blacklisters. Fly back to Hollywood and demand your precious Oscar."

Taylor spoke closely to Susan. "Let me tell you about Victor Hertzig. He's always operating, making every minute pay off. He's at parties like a man with a Geiger counter prospecting for uranium. Everybody gets potted; Victor only *acts* it. He's been slugging tumblers of soda with just enough Scotch to color the drink." He wheeled

52

to address Hertzig directly now. "How much loot were you promised if you could deliver the story?"

"Five thousand dollars." Hertzig chose not to be artful. "But I must produce direct quotes—that was stipulated." He sucked in his lips and said wistfully now, "It's hardly a secret—you'd only be revealing what is pretty generally known."

Taylor laughed harshly. "You can't steal from a man, then beg it from him. Play on his sense of charity."

Susan said, "Alec, dear, don't be so rude."

Hertzig smiled gratefully to Susan. "Invective is Alec's forte. His fortunes have changed, but it's the same sharp tongue. Alec still despises everybody."

"He's now recruiting you as an ally in his game." There was a patronizing quality in Taylor's tone. "Which illuminates another classic Hertzig tactic. If you can't make a direct kill, then level the victim with the connivance of his wife, mistress, mother, best friend, priest."

"But I'm not sure Victor doesn't make good sense," Susan said timidly. "Why *not* claim your Oscar, boldly and openly?"

Hertzig said warmly and at once, "Of course claim it. Confusion to your enemies—expose the whole hypocrisy of it!"

Susan saw Taylor's flaming look, and said nervously, "I meant, if you really are Lester Gates."

"I'm damned glad you tacked on that postscript." Taylor held Susan's eyes intensely. "Baby, you push over like a country milkmaid in a hayloft. I warned you about Victor!"

Susan flushed. "You're being horrible."

Hertzig said, "Club people with words—shame and degrade them. That's Alec."

Taylor laughed loudly, then said generally, "Think Victor Hertzig really gives a damn about any principles or issues involved?" He shook his head. "All words with Victor, dust in your eyes. His way of getting the subject launched, so he can perhaps trick or trap me into an admission."

"Pray God I never need a character reference from Alec Taylor!" Hertzig said it as an invocation, with his eyes heavenward.

"Or a script," Taylor shot back. "You'll rot a long time waiting for that too." He motioned his glass at Susan. "That's Machiavelli's *other* reason for showing up here. He hopes to shoot an indie movie, on location here in Mexico. He's been promised financing, but on condition that he gets *me* to do an original screenplay."

"Not *so* original," Hertzig bargained at once. "I already have the story idea. Your job mainly is to put it into screenplay form." He avoided Taylor's baleful look by turning to Susan. "Two, three weeks' work at the most. It's something Alec could write in his sleep."

Susan said slowly, "Alec has been at loose ends this month. . . ."

Taylor rasped, "You're in the hay with Victor again!"

Susan said angrily. "Alec, *stop* it. You know you work best when you have a definite project and a deadline. You *told* me."

Hertzig said, "Alec sees everybody and everything with a jaundiced eye." He spread his palms. "I've been abused and insulted for nothing. Just for being myself, Victor Hertzig, a man Alec is unreasonably prejudiced against."

"A slob opportunist and a double-dealer," Taylor said scathingly. "I've had dealings with you, Victor—I'm still holding your worthless paper."

Taylor spoke facing Susan, with a finger pointed accusingly at Hertzig. "He once buncoed me into flying to Barcelona at my own expense. Goosed me with a lie about a million-dollar budget, and a British Technicolor commitment. I spent two months in the Ritz Hotel breaking my hump over a screenplay—a damned costume drama about Queen Victoria he was going to film in Spain, with Franco contributing the sound stages gratis."

Taylor's fist raised over Hertzig like a club. "The upshot of it was Victor didn't have a kopeck *or* the commitment he claimed. He'd gotten me to write a script, so he could speculate with it—promote himself into a deal!"

Hertzig said glibly, "An unfortunate coincidence made the project unfeasible. Korda was already making a Technicolor movie about Queen Victoria. Consequently my backers withdrew."

"You lying bastard!" Taylor got the bottle and poured himself a hooker. "I had to bum my way home from Barcelona. Victor didn't even hang around long enough to apologize—he ran like a thief."

Hertzig spoke to Susan. "The story from the writer's point of view. The *true* facts are quite different—but I won't defend myself. It happened yesterday—let it be forgotten." There was a vagrant grin. "A producer is always a bum to a writer."

"Producer?" Taylor's mouth drew in disgust. "Name me one film that hasn't been seized for debt, even before the final cut."

"I've had my share of hard luck," Hertzig said dolefully. He hunched his shoulders. "The small entrepreneur in a monopolistic society—as a Socialist, you should be more sympathetic, Alec."

"I'm only nauseated," Taylor said. "Hertzig class-angling his larcenies, what a laugh! You've got Karl Marx turning over in his grave."

Hertzig wore a look of pain for Susan. "He's neurotic at my expense. As if I'm to blame for his troubles."

Taylor grasped Susan's wrist. "In case you're climbing to that hayloft again—sorry for Victor, and mad at me for mistreating him. About that screenplay he *hopes* I'll do—get this. I'm to do it for pretzels!"

Hertzig said quickly, "For fifteen hundred dollars."

Taylor said, "And in the dark—no screen credit. My pledge in blood that I'll keep the secret."

Hertzig said, "With Alec Taylor's name on it, I couldn't get a major release. There'd be picket lines outside the theaters."

Taylor tapped a finger at Susan. "Stand that against the mock speech he made exhorting me to go pick up my Oscar!"

"Those were the conditions imposed on me." Hertzig avoided Susan's eyes. "I have backers to satisfy—I have no prerogatives in the matter." He continued now in wilting tones, as if already tasting failure. "I offer Alec a chance to pick up some change, and also do me a great favor. A favor I swear to God I'll reciprocate." He met Susan's eyes now. "He's got expenses and no income—how can fifteen hundred dollars hurt him?"

Taylor said, "I sweated blood fifteen years climbing into the forty-thousand-dollar class."

"You're sweating bullets in exile. You don't write, you'll lose your craft." Hertzig nodded to his thesis. "A writer must write. Even for a penny a word—the payment is immaterial."

Susan was looking smilingly at Hertzig. Taylor said disgustedly, "You're not up in that hayloft again!"

Susan laughed. "I've caught on to Victor's method."

Taylor made a mock show of clapping hands. "Wisdom at long last, hooray."

"But a writer must write." She managed to touch the sore only lightly.

Taylor said heavily, "Amen. A writer must, but not for Victor Hertzig." He poured a drink, downed it, then stared moodily at Hertzig. "*No* script, Victor—not a chance in the world. I'd sooner slit my throat. I'm on the beach, but not dead enough for vultures to begin feasting." He smiled thinly. "About that *other* opportunity, you're S.O.L. there too. I make the same statement on it I've made up to now. I neither affirm nor deny that I am alias Lester Gates." He laughed mirthlessly. "Bad business to admit I'm Gates. Certain producers could never again take a chance on me. As a matter of fact, they'd be drummed out of Hollywood. Trust the hundred-and-one-percent patriots for that."

Hertzig poured a stiff drink and held it under Taylor's eyes. "To your father," he toasted, then managed the drink in one swallow.

"My sainted father." Taylor smiled peculiarly. "I was six when I met him for the first time. He lay on a hammock under mosquito netting shaped like a tent. A voluptuary with milk-breasts big as a nursing mother's. There was a tattoo on his chest, down near the diaphragm, a plumed cockatoo in hot, tropical colors that flew at you as my father breathed, heaving his chest. A huge Negro wearing a single earring stood over him waving a straw fan to cool the air." He held his glass up to study reflections of light, then looked at Hertzig and Susan to gauge their interest. "I watched sweat from the Negro fall to my father, drop on drop. This was in the Panama Canal Zone. My mother'd hopefully dragged from Chicago to there, with me as an offering. He'd abandoned her during pregnancy. Her gamble was that the sight of me, a son, his own flesh, would cozen and sucker him, fill him with longings for home and hearth, finally give Mother that sway over him she wanted so terribly."

Taylor balanced his glass on the flat of his palm. "Mother didn't make out. My father would not be roped. He either knew about her, or guessed about her—what she planned for him, the daily come-uppance and persecution." He laughed grimly.

"At home after that, through the months and years, before a pick-up jury of aunts, uncles, cousins and neighbors, we conducted a family trial of my father. With Mother as chief complainant, prosecutor and judge. As her womanhood wasted, and a trickling of remittances came postmarked Honolulu, Hong Kong, Calcutta, wherever, Mother's language got dirty and dirtier. A violence against my father in absentia, his image befouled and effigy-murdered. I was to hate him. As the loyal son of my mother, I must succeed her as chief complainant, prosecutor, judge and hangman."

Taylor stopped, seeing Susan's open embarrassment.

Hertzig said critically, "Words in the air. Put it down on paper, once and for all write that book about your father." He smiled warmly. "You owe it to Society; for all the ears you have bent about your father, you have this debt."

Taylor said, "I was an undergraduate when I came to a decision about that huge Negro I'd watched fanning my father. The Negro was a hermaphrodite."

Susan sounded a shocked outcry, and Taylor's mouth twisted into a smile. He went on with his reminiscence, now ignoring her look that begged him to stop. "My father came home to attend my mother's funeral. It was midwinter, a January frost with ice so thick the pallbearers kept skidding and falling despite the over-coating of coal ash on the walks and paths. My father avoided the church services, but came to stand grave-side as the coffin was lowered. He wore no overcoat in the bitter cold. He wore a tropical suit, tight around his flab like mummy gauze, a pongee shirt and bow tie, a straw hat, and ridiculous brown-and-white shoes pointed like spear heads, with side vents in them. Oh, yes, and a boutonnière, a blue button of a flower that looked artificial."

Taylor laughed, a rowdy burst as if mocking Susan's shocked eyes. "After the burial, my father took me to a saloon. I drank ginger ale, and he downed six whiskeys, neat, in that way he had. He remarked about my mother that she'd been a fine woman, only that and nothing else said about her. He asked me if I hated him, and I said that I did not, not a bit. He said generally that travel was really a bore, but that the habit had taken hold and he could not break it—ever settle into any one place and settle down. He gave me an ancient gold coin and an ornamented silver pillbox. He asked me how old I was, and I told him I was fourteen. When we parted outside the saloon, I watched him walk to a taxi stand and get into a cab. An easy stride to him, as if he hadn't had all those drinks, and impervious to the biting cold, as if he had his own tropical sun somewhere on his person. When the taxi took off, I knew I'd never see him again. Later that night, in my aunt's home, where I'd gone to live, I realized that I'd misstated my age to my father—and that he had either not known or not bothered to correct me. I was actually *seventeen*, not fourteen."

Susan spoke into the silence. "Did you make it up, Alec? I mean, *some* of it?" There was a little-girl incredulity and pleading in her tone.

Taylor said brusquely, "It's fiction." He winked to Hertzig. "It's all fiction, and to hell with it."

Hertzig said, "It's case history, *with* embroidery. Alec is equal parts man and writer. And so mixed together you can't separate them." He smiled. "Pity the analyst who ever gets Alec for a patient!"

Susan said slowly, "But you described a boutonnière, an artificial flower. Can a detail like that be remembered so sharply? Besides, there's a ridiculous quality to all of it." She shook her head quickly, remorsefully. "I mean, it has no reality. It was like something you *dream*."

Hertzig said waggishly, "You have a new innocent, Alec, a fresh captive with big eyes and ears for your remi-niscences. Pour yourself into her, my friend, make her an addict like how many others?"

Susan looked coldly at Hertzig. "I'm not really so much the ingénue, and I resent being patronized. I've had some experience; I have my own sophistication."

Hertzig said mildly, "But Alec nevertheless baffles you.

He's rare in your experience—you don't know what to make of him."

"Not this side of him," Susan said grudgingly. "I'm aware that Alec is complex, but—" She stopped and sighed, looking uneasily at Taylor.

Hertzig kissed her cheek. "I was an innocent once, and then Alec tired of talking to me." He grinned at Taylor. "Words in the air, the macabre exhibits in the secret Taylor museum." He dropped his bantering tone. "What made you reject psychoanalysis, or is it an old question and I've forgotten?" He made his characteristic gesture. "I mean, of course, when you were young enough to profit from analysis."

Taylor sighted Hertzig through slitted eyes, as if bringing him to target. "What did how many years of psychoanalysis accomplish for you?"

"I learned to live with my neurosis," Hertzig shot back promptly.

"Rationalization ad absurdum. Come off it, Victor. You're a disabled little man, even more futile for your time on the couch." Taylor laughed disagreeably. "You should sue for a refund of your money, plus damages."

Hertzig grinned cheerfully, in that patent defense he had against bullies and bullyragging.

Taylor said, "Answering your question now: I simply never found a psychiatrist who could qualify with me." He watched Hertzig's grin broaden, saw the producer's eyes alert Susan to listen.

Taylor said, "For me, a really qualified psychiatrist must experientially have been a thief, panderer, rapist, homosexual, cannibal, murderer." A smile stopped below his eyes. "Not necessarily in the order named. *And* a paranoidal personality, provenly psychotic, with an impressive stay in an insane asylum to his credit." The smile was in his eyes now, and he looked to Hertzig, then to Susan, then back to Hertzig. "I never found a doctor who qualified on all counts, or even a reasonable approximation of them."

Hertzig said, "Trust Alec to give you an answer that is not an answer."

"I think there *was* a value in the answer, only exaggerated." Susan's brow puckered thoughtfully. "Alec was really saying that only a sinner can have true compassion for another sinner, the truest insight—" She looked eagerly to Taylor for agreement.

"Somebody please blow a whistle." Taylor made a face. "We're beginning to sound nauseatingly like a discussion group."

Hertzig said softly, "I respect you, Alec. I disagree with you, but I respect you."

Taylor laughed. "One honest-to-goodness hooker and you're crocked."

Hertzig embraced Taylor, and his eyes dampened. "They're all back working. Ed Storch, Burnside, Cy Gardner, Mitchell Wolfe. The hottest Reds are now respectable Republicans!"

Taylor said, "Some guys were born to live on their knees."

"The only Untouchable left is Alec Taylor." Hertzig said rhetorically, almost chanting, "Can Alec Taylor be rehabilitated and restored to the fold?" He shook his head. "Impossible. He has too many unforgiving enemies. He was the most outrageous radical of them all."

Taylor set up a drink for the producer. "You improve with drink, Victor!"

Hertzig stumbled into an embrace with Susan. "Say that you love Alec Taylor," he commanded.

Susan said, "I love Alec Taylor."

"Why?" There was a comical set to Hertzig's jaw.

"Well, he's colorful, tragic, talented, mad, outspoken—"

Hertzig shook his head wildly. "I mean, give me his virtues as a lover!"

Susan's cheeks reddened and she turned away from the producer. When she saw Taylor's eyes on her, she met his amused gaze steadily, saying nothing. When Taylor turned to the bar, she tried desperately to prevent that inside flooding of shame and self-reproach that had developed in this last week of her intimacy with him. She'd watched the slow unraveling of him, the slow exposure, a frightening metamorphosis, as if she'd gone to bed with one man and had awakened to another. The picture it made for her was those awesome camera transitions as the soul etched itself horribly on the face, as the movie Dr. Jekyll became the movie Mr. Hyde.

She'd misunderstood his melancholia, let herself be compelled by it because she was driven by her own. She'd walked meltingly into his fire, only to know greater cold.

She looked broodingly at Taylor, noting that bodily suggestion of a man contracting in his clothes, as if about to jump, explode in all directions. She sighed heavily. *Anyhow, he exhausted her.* There was too much to explore, too much to him; and in the exploration of him, she could only further lose herself, that urgent self-exploration she had only lately attempted. And the intimacy she gave he took as tribute, that added drop to an already overflowing bucket.

It had no consequence, none for him, anyhow. And it had no more consequence for her, not truly, than those other frantic times when in escape from herself, she'd run full into herself.

A mental picture gripped her now, caught terribly at her imagination. That Taylor was a mirror held up to her own sickness. That the charge of violence in him, and his disorder, had been the magnet, his attraction for her. She'd not been drawn to the man so much as to his hell. So the lamps in his would light both their hells.

I wasn't really the susceptible female, she told herself now, or the matron abroad so starved for sex mementos. I wasn't really so beguiled or specially charmed by Alec, or deceived into anything. In this fight for myself, this awful need for self-realization, I deliberately took a man to bed, and was taken to bed. I now find him too overpowering and mad, because I am still weak and not quite so mad.

Taylor stared intensely at the forest of whiskey bottles on the bar. As the bottles grew in his eye with all else eclipsed, he set them to dancing. They were cartoon animations now, fat-bellied, with gazelle necks. Soon the choreography became frantic, a melee of loose-jointed spastics bumping each other with crashing effect.

He wondered vaguely how much he had drunk. Ten, or was it times two? He had this god-awful tolerance for the stuff, as if it was so much water. He had no way of gauging his consumption, never those telling symptoms of disequilibrium or thickened speech. The stuff soaked into him as if his insides were a massive sponge. He stored the stuff as if it were the fuel that made him go; his kidneys were a tank with reserve compartments, and the stoppers welded into place.

He stood with his back to Susan, but aware of her, acute to some pressure of her against him, his name in her thoughts. He smiled secretly to himself. For days now, he'd sensed Susan's dilemma, the banal and obsessive self-auditing, the great, raging, moral debate with the two sides of Susan in locked battle.

Two sides that added up to half a woman.

He refurbished those scenes in which she'd auditioned for him, so he could rate her, decide how much he wanted to invest in her. No script—Susan drawing only from sense memory, her accumulated womanhood. He'd acted with her, but had also stood away looking on.

He shook his head to the scenes and quickly struck the sets.

Soppy, mawkish theater; too much the extract of maudlin reality. The dialogue was embarrassingly cliché, out of confession magazines; the passions summoned and the articulation of them too frenetic, too fey, too falsetto, too orchestrated. Susan was egregiously still the neophyte, pubescent and troubled by her sex; lovemaking never raised up from the bog of petting.

Taylor shrugged apathetically. He was hardly involved, he had made no real investment. He'd been clinician more than lover, a meter recording decibels of groans, moans, cries.

All unusable as story—even Marie Corelli or Laura Jean Whosis would get a turn-down on it today.

He wrote the obituary to love in his mind, having fun with it. *A love chapter of blank pages.* He tried his skill at an alliterative one-liner built around a lewd word, but after some fumbling he gave up on it.

He turned now to face Susan. Their eyes met and they

smiled to each other. As if having made their mutual good-bys in their thoughts, they could now perhaps better enjoy those moments and days that were yet to be spent together.

10

Harding had the emotion of prowling, walking lightly on the balls of his feet, all of him contracted against that sudden challenge of some hidden guard that every nerve in him was anticipating. He'd come to the Villa de la Soledad on foot, straight from the Galería Tajín.

The ground-level corridors of the villa depressed and baffled him; his memory revived that time in the catacombs of Rome when he'd lost Susan for almost a half-hour. Memory touched, too, the haunted interiors he had once viewed in a TV pilot film screened privately for Brant, Bellows, Appleby and Harding. What's it again? Mmmmm, *Foreign Intrigue.*

He wondered about the informality of the front door— why no bell or buzzer, or butler? And why no cashier's booth charging admission to museum visitors, he thought to himself. The place to his eye so far was a warehouse of relics, art folderol, junk antiques. The stuff Appleby's dipso wife was always dragging home to Chappaqua from Manhattan's auction rooms. He paused briefly to gawk at a wall of murals, done in encaustic, that depicted milk-white angels and dimpled cherubs, various biblical scenes of Creation.

He had an amusing thought about the villa now. It was that ultimate heaven reserved specially for auctioneers, and served the thieving bastards right. He peered closely at one angel's face in the close foreground of a mural panel, comparing it with something he'd spied somewhere before, a painting that hung on the wall behind the home bar in Appleby's den. A nude on a couch, attributed to the painter Bouguereau—a twin to this one, face-wise if not in the general upholstery. He nodded to the angel, and spoke irreverently in his mind. *I've seen you with your wings clipped, lady.*

Harding chuckled to himself, and expanded the bit. If Mildred Appleby were here now, she'd bid you up to five hundred dollars, and then load you in the station wagon. Mildred's a procurer for Appleby, every naked lady in print, chromo or oil she can find. To titillate old Appleby, rescue him from impotence.

He heard some sounds now, voices and music coursing at him as through a long tunnel, and he reversed his direction. Moving back along the wall of mural, he stopped suddenly with a nervous start. He stared incredulously at the detail of the painting that was the whiskered prophet Isaiah in a loose cloth robe, and blinked his eyes as if dispelling an optical delusion. He saw it move, mahogany-brown, with long feelers, strange as some thing from prehistory. He finally identified it as a *cucaracha*, huge and loathsome, a common pest in the warm, damp climate of Mexico.

When he found the salon, Harding's quick impulse was to cover his face and steal away as he'd come. He suddenly felt like the interloper he was, not up to the bravura and sham the next minutes demanded. His emotion was to postpone the routing out of Susan, trade this day in for tomorrow, get a night's sleep and revamp his sales logic for what might be a harder sell than hitherto. He'd come a very long way, he was bushed physically, his morale at low ebb from all the flogging thoughts and fears.

Scram, Harding, was the whispering in his brain. You're edgy right now and demoralized, look like a bum off the road. In the shape you're in, you couldn't sell a vacuum cleaner if you threw in a Cadillac as a bonus premium. Besides, the element of surprise is too great. Much smarter to put Susan on notice, not just drop out of the blue. She's over twenty-one, entitled to be treated as an adult and equal—hasn't that been her hue and cry? You're only setting her up for that same speech damning your proprietary attitudes, the roughshod trampling of her rights and prerogatives. *Bug off, Harding,* now, before somebody spots you and it's too late. Take a room in town and phone Susan from there. Set up a date for tomorrow, give her at least that much equality in this.

He looked into the salon and formed a quick impression of it. *One of those,* he thought. Stand-up drinking nose to nose, and smoke until your eyeballs burned. Talk, ack-ack into deaf ears; your non-listening partner picking through his own repertory of clichés, impatient for his turn center-stage. And come drunkenness, come bathos. Drowning eyes and the crying towel. All children of God now, in a community tub of tears. Scrub my soul, lover, and I'll, hic, wash the mud off you. We're all brothers and sisters in this parlous world, one obscenity family of man, so, hic, please, no shame. Unzip outside and in, down to the marrow.

The unvarying cocktail party, in Mexico, Fairfield County, Southampton, Park Avenue, wherever.

Harding was still stalling doubtfully just outside the salon when the decision was made for him. The guests were to a man staring at him, like an audience in drill attention to an actor's entrance. He nodded to the room in an easy assurance he did not feel, and then saw Susan coming toward him. Susan looking more like a snapshot of herself in an early time of their marriage than the worn picture of her he carried in his mind. And, most remarkably, with no visible show of surprise on her face, or obvious resentment, over the sudden sight of him.

They came together, and Harding nervously held out a hand in greeting. They shook hands lightly; the first handshake in their fifteen years of courtship, marriage, divorce.

Harding grinned foolishly. "Feels funny shaking hands with your wife."

Susan did not correct him, did not put their relationship into its right tense, and Harding took courage from this. "I traced you from Mexico City to here. It took some ingenuity."

Susan smiled wisely. "It also took some bribes."

He nodded cheerfully. "Sure, that too. I had to loosen some tongues. You'd covered your tracks pretty good."

"Richard, you missed your trade."

He winked to show he got it. "Harding, pride of the force."

Susan looked at him with solemn eyes. "It's over, Richard. Done and finished. Please don't make it sticky."

He stared closely at her now, struck by a fresh, new quality in her. "Know something? You look ten years younger!"

Her eyes lighted. "I've been feeling so good. For the first time in ages."

He said, with a damp look, "We'll talk it over. Straight and honest. No digs, no meanness." He looked closely at her, really trying to pinpoint for himself those changes she'd effected. "Now I get what you've done. You've cut your hair short, lopped off ten or so pounds."

"Lopped off *twenty-two* pounds."

"Hey, was that so smart? You know your tendency to anemia." There was a flashing look of worry. "When was the last medical checkup?"

Susan said, with helpless, bubbling laughter, "You haven't by any chance got my Feosol pills with you!"

"They're home in the medicine chest." His eyes shone. "Who worries about you like I do?"

Encouraged by the light mood, Harding said, "The house looks like Tobacco Road. I've got the cat boarding with the MacKenzies."

Her face changed at once, and she said icily, "And how are our children, Richard, Junior, and the twins?"

Harding said, "That was pretty cheap. I miss not having kids as much as you do."

She said forbiddingly, "We're divorced. I'm finally and at last your ex-wife. Please get it through your head."

"If I believed that, I wouldn't have flown out here."

"Richard, it's so!"

"A phony Mexican divorce. They pass them out on the streets like handbills. Susan, be sensible!"

Her face clouded. "Then you came to make trouble, to devil me with technicalities."

"I came to iron matters out—let you know how much you mean to me."

She said angrily, "Serve your own precious ego, and never mind about my feelings!"

"Hey, how'd we get into this god-awful vein?" He looked around nervously. "Damned if we're not being stared at."

Harding's eyes fixed on Alec Taylor in the salon, bobbing woozily where the portable bar was. He noted Taylor's informal garb, the open sandals, the stiff, pine-needle bed of hair, the muscled stance of a male model posing in the nude.

Harding's mouth crooked in quick, intuitive dislike, and he characterized Taylor in his mind. Crap artist and poseur, either a writer or a painter. The dirty-underwear type—has a collection of off-beat opinions, mainly for its shock value, and to call attention to himself. Doesn't believe in God or man, only in himself.

He faced Susan again, and said in dropped tones, "Just telling me off isn't enough, Susan. After fifteen years, I want more of a story. Even if it's a showdown, a wrap-up for keeps. I'll give up, and for good, the moment you've convinced me." He offered his hand. "I give you my promise on that."

Susan ignored his hand. "Richard, you're *acting* for all you're worth. In your own boorish way mocking at me, and us. Deep down, you really don't feel a thing, or care a hoot."

He frowned darkly. "That's a hell of a thing to say."

"I've been gone for seven weeks. Just *when* did you begin to miss me!"

"Why, right away." He sought answers in his mind now, as honest as he could find. "Sure, I let time slide by. You were simply on a vacation, that's how I rationalized it. You'd come home the better for it."

"But you *knew* I'd filed for divorce. Richard, you were notified."

He said doggedly, "They wrap tortillas in divorce papers out here. I wasn't too worried." He sought to smile. "You were on a kick, and I didn't want to spoil it. Like I'd spoiled it those other times." He edged closer to her now, his eyes tender. "It doesn't take much for an old married couple to dump a divorce."

She drew away, as if into cover. "If I told you that I'm involved with somebody—" She saw his look of immediate hurt and nodded at him. "It's so, Richard."

A moment later Harding found the resource to smile bleakly. "You really walloped me!"

"I hoped not to have to tell you. Since it's none of your business anyhow."

He stared at her. "You really felt as free as that!"

Her mouth drew into a tight line. "If that's an oblique way of calling me a tramp."

He said in a sickly tone, "We've really got ourselves a situation."

"I asked you before not to make it sticky."

He was back to staring critically at her. "That damned

hard quality in you, Susan. How in God's name did you hide it all these years?"

"Richard, give up and go home. Now."

He shook his head. "A rebound affair—I've heard of those." He tried to smile. "I honestly never thought you'd be susceptible. . . . But what man thinks his wife is?" He brooded silently, and then said, "It won't hurt forever. I say to hell with it."

She said derisively, "Which of the agency's soap operas did that gem of dialogue come from?"

"It came from my guts." He shook his head. "You keep roughing me up, clobbering me. What for, Susan?"

She had the answer for him at once. "The way people lie, to others and to themselves. How a whole life can be lived out without one moment of truth. Does that answer you?"

"No, it doesn't. I don't understand a word of it."

"Of course not. We see fifteen years differently, just as we lived them differently." Her eyes on him were mocking. "But I'm still being too obscure for your practical mind!"

Harding kept silent. He felt suddenly inept, futile and foolish. He stared uneasily at her, for the first time knowing their estrangement. Her eyes on him were cold and flat, nothing of their past mirrored in them that he could see. As if she'd substituted new eyes for the old ones, along with cutting her hair, streamlining her figure, transforming from the jellied matron look to the sleek *jeune fille* silhouette.

He'd come to repossess her, but he hadn't done enough homework, dug into the shambles of their marriage, to dis-

73

cover where the materials had been lacking. While he'd sat on his brains in the offices of Brant, Bellows, Appleby and Harding, Susan had given the two months to investigating the shambles, and then to saving herself. Saving herself, and building a coffin for him. He'd arrived in Mexico just as she was nailing down the lid.

His gaze strayed into the salon again, lingering over Donna Flores, photographing faces, forming impressions. He saw a stubby, bald fellow holding a brandy snifter over near the hi-fi, and frowned trying to decide whether the man was Russian or German, and what made his face seem so familiar. He saw Alec Taylor at the bar, and a thought knifed through him. Was this bohemian slob the man of the hour with Susan? He looked as if he could quote from Freud, make rape seem natural and inevitable.

Harding began to sag inside as the task confronting him grew enormously in his mind. He was in for a fight, with all the weapons in Susan's hand, her greatest weapon being her remarkable uninterest in him. *Unless* it was all an act, he thought now in a small rise of hope. A feigned uninterest, to get the man down on his knees—Susan using that most ancient of feminine tricks.

Now hope surged higher. The lover, too, was surely a myth. No such animal—just one more cunning device to get his bowels in an uproar, beat him to the ground, retaliate against him for her own wounded vanity, the bad times he'd given her.

Self-buoyed now, Harding nodded to himself. Some women put out, others never. Susan was notoriously proper, stuck with a too-rigid moral code. No sneaked kisses; no guy ever got one solitary free feel at parties. Harding smiled reminiscently—he'd gotten complaints over it. More than one amorous party lush had felt Susan's claws in close quarters.

Harding said almost serenely, "Susan, I need a drink."

Susan said, "Then you insist on punishing yourself."

"Whatever that means." He smiled. "Can't just wrap up a life and toss it into the trash can. There are certain civilized rituals—we're not insects or apes." He reached to take her arm. "What's your hostess' attitude on free loaders?"

Susan permitted him her arm. "It's Sunday open house. My hostess likes people, the more the merrier. And the more celebrated, the better." There was a sarcastic note. "You'll qualify beautifully. Just be sure to name-drop Brant, Bellows, Appleby and Harding."

Harding said blithely, heartened now and with some of his confidence restored, "We'll sell the house first thing— who needs it! Too damned isolated, and you're stuck with the same faces like we're all of us squatting in one life-boat." He squeezed her arm. "We'll find an apartment in town, spend more time together as a result. I never want to see a commuter's train."

He squeezed her arm fervently, emboldened now by his first success. "Maybe we'll even adopt a baby. Go abroad for one, if we can't make it with the adoption agencies here."

Susan burst into laughter.

"What's so funny?" Harding asked.

"Your way of saying things. It all sounds soapy to me, like 'Young Doctor Malone' and 'John's Other Wife.' "

Harding couldn't stifle his sudden anger. "You keep beating me with Madison Avenue. But I've never once heard you say no to money, *Mrs.* Harding."

11

The rooms upstairs were huge and stood to but one side of the structure, as if in the century and a half, by some freak tropism, they had been drawn to the sun. There were only archways and no connecting doors, and what detachment each room had from the others was realized by an oddity of short, boxlike corridors constructed in ingenious twists and turns. The upper-level terrace that nuzzled into the sheer bluff sat outside four of the rooms, and was accessible from all four through glass-bead-curtain doors.

The sounds in one room coursed to all the others, but unintelligibly, with the echo effect of voices diluted and diminished through a funnel.

In one of the rooms, Lisa Franke was posed before a gold-painted dressing table, in enamoured study of the image she saw, like a sculptor tooling at a bust, to prod the clay here to raise the breast, work meticulously there to fix the eye into an almond look. The mirrored image was eye-catching, for beauty, and that provocative agelessness. The skin, where it showed nude to the hips, was smooth, nut-brown in its even tan, and remarkably flat over the diaphragm. The breasts were high, as if wired under the skin, and the nipples thrust out stiffly.

She tested the image for its smile, and then, satisfied with the brilliant white of it and the naturalness, she selected one

76

perfume from the nest of bottles on the vanity top. She dabbed at her hair with the dampened stopper, then under both armpits and in her cleavage. She had the stopper mid-motion to other anatomy when the sounds in the next room finally distracted her from herself.

She'd been half-hearing them for some time, but with no acute register of the sounds—a droning in her ears, with hardly a definition of voice, no word clearly overheard.

She stood irresolutely for a moment, in some inner struggle, then she stepped carefully out of her mules, to walk with cat's feet through an archway and stand quietly in the corridor closest to the next room. She was sharp-eared now, attuned like any eavesdropper to the sounds she heard. Her face was subtly changed: cracks in the mask of paint, the lips pursed, and furrows in her wide, flat brow. She looked as if she had little taste for what she was doing, yet was for some reason driven to it, and at a cost in self-esteem.

Just around the L of the corridor where Lisa stood, a man lay curled fetus-like in a heart chair. He was Ed Fowler, christened Edward John. His skin looked peculiar, mottled where the copper tan had faded, and with tiny vein bursts from some ordeal of breathing. Sweat beaded his brow, stained the front of his blue silk pajamas. A hand was over his heart, the fingers busy in a light caressing massage, done in an automatic, nervous way; the hand self-powered, and his brain unaware of it.

He was listening intently to Harry Archer, a snout-nosed, bespectacled fellow with thick, swollen lips, who was sitting chair-side. Fowler's eyes were wary and mistrustful, his mouth a single hard line—the characteristic look of a defendant in the dock steeled against the prosecutor's gambit.

Archer suddenly stopped his harangue, took off his eyeglasses and wiped the fog off the lenses. His tone apologized. "I laid it on you, and maybe a little too much." He peered near-sightedly at Fowler. "You're mad, huh?"

"Pissed off. What did you expect, Harry?" A muscle jumped in Fowler's cheek. "I didn't ask you all the way out here to put me back on trial—rehash all the old crap." For a moment, his hand stopped its automatic massage. "What prompted it—what in hell was it for?"

"So you'd know the *size* of the job you're asking me to do. I'm a public-relations man, Ed, not a miracle worker." Archer gestured to encompass the surroundings. "You've been away a long time, you've forgotten a lot. The natural thing for you to do was to try to forget." He shook his head. "But the public hasn't forgotten—don't kid yourself that they have."

Archer reached down to strike knuckles hard against a diplomat's case. "I've got proof of that in here. A press file covering your years away—I had my office compile it for me. You're topical, *still*." His knuckles struck the case again. "Not *one* solitary word in them favorable to you, the *least bit* sympathetic. They're still hanging you in effigy back home." He nodded somberly at Fowler. "Time hasn't improved your situation a bit. They even made a comedy of your latest heart attack. Blame yourself, Ed. You didn't cross the border into obscurity. You merely exchanged one limelight for another"—there was a hectoring note now—"as if you were too vain to do the intelligent thing, too much the egotist."

Fowler said resentfully, "What was I supposed to do? Crawl into a hole and die?"

Archer smiled faintly. "You had more choices than *two*. The fact is, you've been living and disporting yourself here in Mexico like a feudal lord. Elegant houses, flashy women, a show of wealth." He shook his head. "All wrong, very ill-advised. You provided ammunition for critics at home; even alienated what few supporters you had."

Fowler was momentarily withdrawn. Soon he spoke in explosive bursts, from some deep, hoarded agony. "*Thirty years* in public service—God, is there a price to it! Harry, have you any idea how much living a man postpones because of a public career?"

"There were compensations in it, Ed. Or you wouldn't have made the sacrifices, or the compromises." The shoulders hunched. "Anyhow, you chose your own bed."

Fowler said, "There's that Big Eye on you all the time. The Voter all the time wondering whether he made a bad buy—whether he ought to swap you in, or junk you." Fowler painfully lifted himself up from the chair and balled one hand into a fist. "You can't take a leak that somebody isn't checking to see if you're doing it in the ladies' toilet. A rabble horde of hypocrites and crackpots keeping a daily diary on you, just waiting to catch you in one human vice!"

Fowler eased back in the heart chair, his fingers once more in that voodooism with his heart, estimating how much more expenditure he dared. He said, "All right, you play it shrewd and discreet, you do what's required of you. You mouth pieties, kiss babies, feed caviar to Callahan's cat, you love and adore everybody. You're a churchgoer, fine fellow, fine husband, goddam eunuch. You've got a double zipper on your fly, and a padlock on the zipper. You're living in a glass house, so please, no indecent exposure."

The voice raised a decibel. "But you're a loser anyhow, Harry—because nobody believes what they see. You look and sound too good, much too saintly, the record is *too* clean. Now the mud-slingers and character assassins begin on you. A whisper here, a word there, and quick as quick, you're tarred to the eyeballs. You're suddenly a phony and a fraud, a front for the interests, a front for the gangs. Plus that, the word's out that you're a secret bottle baby, sex hound and crook."

Archer said, "You're wet to the skin. Better get into dry clothes."

Fowler said furiously, "Hear me, Harry—I've been waiting years to air my side of it!" His voice was more in his throat now, and his chest rose and fell. "About the time of my troubles, a slob of a senator decides to get into the act. He's a come-lately, recently elected; he's got nothing to do but write homey progress letters to his constituents. He's dumb about national issues, in the total dark about foreign affairs. Besides, he'd been warned by the older pros to only listen and behave himself. Keep shut, vote with his party, and wait his turn at a committee job."

Fowler disfigured his mouth. "But the Junior Senator's 'way more ambitious than that. The monotony's got him down—he wants faster action for himself. It was tough getting elected; he loves Washington life. The food's good, the money's great, and he's finally wearing shoes. He never, never wants to leave Washington."

Fowler struck his chest. "*I* become his career insurance

—the vehicle for his big leap onto the front page, close-ups on the home television screen. He doesn't know beans about municipal politics, but he's got bright young investigators who know how to dumb-up a dossier, fob off hearsay as evidence. Getting the go-ahead from his fellow senators is a snap—they're delighted to get him out from underfoot. Now it all begins to roll for Junior, the big road show—*the Senate Investigation into Municipal Crime and Corruption.* He's got built-in theater, a sure-fire hit."

Fowler coughed violently and slumped back into a prone position, curled in the womb of the heart chair again, and somehow more shrunken in it now than before. He said whisperingly, as if for his own ears, "I'm *really* a loser now. I'm chief villain in a crucifixion staged for sixty million howling watchers. My thirty years in public life couldn't count for less if I'd spent them in a paper-box factory."

Fowler rolled onto his side—ghostly pale, his eyes burned-out, and the skin pouches under them lower, as if dripping down to his cheeks. "Slink off to somewhere and live as a penitent? Balls, Harry! Had you ever advised me like that, I'd have spit right in your eye. Sure, I looked bad during the hearings, and I did quit under fire—but I didn't feel guilty, Harry; *at no time did I feel guilty.* Only blazing mad, and goddam martyred. I came here sworn to have some of those kicks I'd missed—live as I damn pleased in *this* glass house, and let peepers beware."

There was a long interval of silence; the sounds only of Fowler's harsh, irregular breathing.

Archer said anxiously, "You're a damned fool getting so steamed up. In your condition."

Fowler fluttered a hand weakly. "Two of those pills; the green bottle, Harry. And some water."

The pills were on a squat, circular teakwood table with an onyx top. *One* green bottle in a pharmaceutical array of powders, restoratives, medicines.

Water was inconveniently in a washroom off the corridor, and Archer went to get it. In the winding corridor, he butted into what felt like a standing stone figure, nude to the waist, in a half-slip that hugged the hips. His eyeglasses fell down his nose, distorting and doubling the size of what he saw. He turned his head away; then when he finally looked again, Lisa had gone off.

He was administering the pills and the water to Fowler when he made the obvious decision about the encounter in the corridor. Lisa had been there eavesdropping.

He puzzled over it for a while, then gave up thinking about it.

Fowler's breathing was more normal now—the emergency, as such, had been bridged. Some color was back in his cheeks; the pills had been an exotic fuel for his bloodstream.

Archer got up, to pace toward the terrace, as a way of marking time. He looked out through the leaded glass, saw the old man in the invalid's chair. He stared with startled eyes at the paint brushes strapped to Max's arms; made startled note of the old man's face. There were only flat planes in it, as if no cheeks; the eyes were extraordinarily deep, as if the sockets were empty. A death's-head—a sight to send shivers up your spine on a bright day.

Fowler was stirring in a reawakening of life, and

Archer went back to sit chair-side again. He gestured foolishly, still in the shock of it. "The old guy out there —who is he, Ed?"

Fowler made a face. "I got the willies myself, the first time I saw him. He's Max Marsant, Lisa's father." He touched his skull. "He's senile. He's out there all day, fooling with paint."

"Is he any good? I mean, as a painter."

Fowler shrugged indifferently. "I wouldn't know. Let's get back to it, Harry."

Archer waited until their eyes met. "I say again, you're asking me to work a miracle."

Fowler said avidly, "A quick miracle!" He added cloudily, "I want to chin with old friends, take in a ball game, walk around, take a last look. Harry, I want to go home, but *not* in a casket."

Archer pursed his lips. "How bad is it?"

"The *second* attack, Harry." Fowler tried to smile. "One more, and I've struck out." He said passionately, "Sure I'm a hard sell. But my faith is, *you* can sell me. Only you, Harry—you're the best. The record says you're the best." A hand found Archer's knee. "Mind you, Harry, I'm not asking for a royal welcome, any red carpet. I just don't want to be clobbered." His face shadowed. "I'd keel over dead if all I came home to was brickbats!"

Archer said slowly and carefully, "I've handled stickers in my time, made people think black was white. But you're something else, Ed—I frankly doubt whether I can pull it off."

Fowler was silent, with begging eyes.

Archer continued, "The campaign's formula enough. The sympathetic build-up. How you scratched and clawed for an education, your Horatio Alger rise, how you never lost the common touch, newspapers please copy. Ed Fowler, the do-gooder and humanitarian, with inspired testimonials certifying same. And with all that, sob copy about your bum heart, how your days are numbered." Archer smiled faintly. "And to cap it, I organize welcome-home banquets for you—pressure certain people to attend, bribe some, blackmail others—"

Fowler said quickly and eagerly, "Do it like that, Harry. I'll underwrite it—I buy it."

Archer shook his head. "The public won't buy it, they'll knock us dead." He held Fowler's eyes and said pointedly, "They still want an answer to the *one* big question."

Fowler said gratingly, "If you ask me, it's in *your* mind, Harry. Solely and exclusively."

Archer said dryly, "Let's keep it friendly."

"You've sat here playing a smooth game of bunco, Harry." Fowler's eyes glinted. "How much loot did Ed Fowler make off with, and how much of it can drop into your lap? Frankly, Harry, hasn't that been uppermost in your mind all the way out here?"

"Excuse me for touching a sore spot." Archer smiled slightly. "I'll let the insult pass. You're a sick man, and full of anxieties."

Fowler said sharply, "You don't have to be clever to make out with me. You want a fat fee, name it."

Archer said "Fifty thousand?" When Fowler nodded, he stipulated, "In front, and in cash—and nothing guaranteed."

"I don't want to die among strangers." Fowler's look was haunted. "I want to go home and die where I belong." He sighed. "Give thirty years to something, you want a few honest tears shed when you go. Damn it, Harry, I rate it, I'm entitled to it."

Archer stared narrowly at Fowler, then said, "You want all the pomp and circumstance—isn't that what you're really after?" The tone was heavy with irony now. "The full treatment, huh, Ed? Body lying in state, flags lowered, lines of mourners, stuff."

Fowler glowered resentfully, "Suppose I do want that—"

Archer laughed. "It's coming to you, huh?"

"Don't kid with me, Harry—or rib me." Fowler's mouth twisted. "You've struck gold in Choluca. Damn it, show a a little gratitude."

After a small silence, Archer said, "You've handed me a job, now I'll hand *you* one—"

"What?"

"Move out of the glass house. And right away. Take a modest flat somewhere away from the jazz." Archer nodded to the question he read in Fowler's look. "Live *alone*." The corners of his mouth tucked in. "Stop being Daddy-O in the gossip columns."

Fowler nodded again. Archer read his watch. "A car's picking me up at eight. There's a midnight plane out of Mexico City."

"Why not spend the night," Fowler said perfunctorily. "Rest up. Get going in the morning."

Archer shook his head. "Can't do. As it is, I'm here on borrowed time. Besides, I'm being married Tuesday morning—or did the big news stop at the border?"

Fowler said at once, "I did read about it." His eyes trained keenly on Archer. "Is it a marriage, or a grab, Harry?"

Archer flushed. He said forbiddingly, "If you're thinking of ribbing me—*don't*."

Fowler said anyhow, having fun with it, "She's buried three husbands so far, and damned profitably." He smiled openly. "Marriage to an addled and elderly widow is a pretty shrewd way of getting into oil, magazine publishing and whatever else. You move into the life enterprises and fortunes of three tycoons, simply by having outlived them!"

Archer had a struggle keeping his temper. "The kettle's calling the pot." His mouth twisted. "Twenty million dollars. Eat your heart out, Ed."

Fowler said provocatively, "*When* you get your hands on it." He watched Archer's eyes. "From the lady's record so far, there's that chance she might add Harry Archer Associates to her holdings."

Archer rasped, "I'm physically sound as a bell! God damn it, Ed—I'm mainly here as a favor. In a minute now, you can take your fee and—" He stopped his speech, again seeking self-possession. He eyed Fowler narrowly for some moments, then said evenly, "You really dislike me, huh, Ed."

Fowler's eyes met Archer's fully. "Who in this world can *you* honestly say you like, Harry?"

12

The old man was aware of Lisa first as a shadow on his canvas, as if the sun had gone behind a cloud. The paint brushes dropped; he slowly brought his hands back to his sides, then maneuvered his wheel chair toward Lisa.

He saw her bare feet first, then his eyes moved up slowly, in a methodical examination of her—done coldly, with his eyes peculiar, as if he somehow saw the form naked and his slitted eyes were knives cutting the whole into chunks for separate exhibit.

He laughed now, in a prelude to his old man's game, a laugh that was no more than a fluttering in the stomach, with no muscles to it. Then his eyes closed, the lids over them thick and scabrous, and the story of it played for him in camera. The personal history of Lisa, as he specially knew it.

The film made moments of decades, one stage of a diverse, world geography. He saw lovers in a mass assembly, then moving one by one into tableau with Lisa. The faces varied: there were Caucasian faces, and the eggshell white of a Member of Parliament; the dark-pigmented, from Mediterranean olive to unmiscegenated black. A yellow face moved from the pack to clasp Lisa in a lover's embrace, and memory imposed a biographic subtitle on the picture Max saw. Lung Sarit Sarasin, a Malayan business-man, owner of newspapers, plantation land and uncounted peons. A face in remotest limbo, one of Lisa's earliest lovers, yet Max saw it vividly, as if the Malayan stood before him right then.

All of them, in their hour, Lisa's patrons; some for her convenience, the many for that other food.

Max stopped the film and visualized Fowler in the bedroom off the terrace. His mouth wreathed in dislike—he found Fowler more loathsome than he'd ever found the others. An uncultivated boor, a self-glutting swine.

He was about to speak, complain to Lisa about his lot, the awful neglect of him, when his chance was suddenly gone. He watched Lisa re-cross the terrace as if still blind to his presence, then vanish through the wide doors.

13

In Fowler's room, Lisa completed the last touches in her dressing. Harry Archer was gone now, off showering and shaving in one of the guest rooms, making ready for his return to Mexico City and his flight from there back to New York.

Fowler watched Lisa silently, with his thoughts mainly

on himself. His eyes were clouded and his hand was on his chest, feeling his heartbeat. There'd been a second attack two weeks before—a sudden dark, with blood flooding his brain and that suffocation of corks in his throat, and his mind stumbling. More severe, with a longer pain for a conscious time, than that first attack three years ago in his native city. He'd fainted dead away then, in temporary death and marvelously anesthetized. A coronary occlusion, he'd been told later; that quirk of human physiology, aggravated by the enormous strains of public office. He'd smiled over the diagnosis then, in his own secret wisdom minimizing it. Diagnosing it for himself, as some other wise fellows had too, as a seizure induced by the shattering logic of fifteen hundred pages of public evidence against his administration. He'd stopped his heart in the perfect dodge; purposely stopped the theater before the final act, and so avoided the verdict. But . . . this second attack now proving the first . . .

His stare followed Lisa, as she held up a heavy necklace of gold pieces, a gradation of coins from antique Guatemalan dollars to British guineas. A fortune of gold, more than its extrinsic worth, that he had bargained away from a peasant, to give as one more gift to Lisa.

He fixed on the contours of her back, the remarkably elastic look that belied her near-fifty years. She wore a peasant skirt with a wide ruffled bottom that fell to her ankles. A white petticoat was the only underwear, and when she stepped into sun areas the hard-rubber mold of her buttocks could be traced. The top was a low-cut cotton blouse with a chain-stitched geometric pattern in bright-colored threads, with armholes in the exact measurements of her arms.

His look became resentful, as the memory of that night stabbed through him once more. He'd lain beside her, lovemaking, when the attack suddenly overcame him. He remembered her look—her face raised over him, molten and awry from her heat—and a hand raised as if to slap his face. Then when she'd understood his emergency, she had done all those dutiful things. But with no actual solicitude for him; her eyes cold and full of censure. As if accusing him for the bed and the hour he'd picked for it, the galling effrontery of him.

She was back at the mirror, fixing the lie of the blouse inside the skirt. She saw Fowler's face in the glass, that blinded look the eyes get when thoughts turn inward. She guessed his thoughts; knew he'd been thinking of nothing else since his attack.

He's reliving the emergency, she told herself. It all died for Fowler that night—his fancy of youth and the giddy illusion gone as his heart expired. *Peculiar old man*, she thought, his mind full-up with smutty jokes and the toilet scribblings of boys. Where was the maturity, the wisdom come of sixty years?

She wondered about his wives now. That one divorced, and that one dead. Had they been women or wood—else how could a man save up so much coarseness? She imaged them disdainfully: automatons with steel corsets and chastity locks, and the vessels through which feeling flowed, refrigerated.

She tried to remember the ancient song Fowler still thrilled to, the one he demanded in night clubs and ballrooms, and paid out money to hear. Yes, "Three O'Clock in the Morning." And that comical waltz he did to the music, with rusted knees and urgent leaps as if treading beds of quicksand.

She covertly stared at his face once more, marveled over the pillaged look to him, watched the ritual of fingers over his heart. Her thoughts resumed, making phrases in her mind. He sees that night as a fall from on high, the burning bulb of his male vanity cruelly extinguished. It was hard for Lisa not to smile—Fowler's fall had been no more than off the lowest step of a ladder to the floor. He'd been half-dead before, ridiculous in his play, inept and selfish in sex, only wanting the aphrodisiac of it.

Lisa shrugged, not caring, only god-damning Fowler in her mind for spoiling the comfortable equilibrium of things. Her pretense with him had been easy, easier for Fowler's money. He'd hardly touched her, unequipped with ideas as he was, and futile even in that which he'd saved up for too long.

Her stare found the wall at the foot of their bower that was the home screen. In her mind, she saw Fowler playing projectionist with inept hands, fuming and cursing when the machine failed. He'd brought the eight-mm. movies from the States, along with other contraband. She winced remembering some of the titles, the outhouse text of them. Had he even saved this up too, she wondered. Or had his wives, secure in their steel, acted indulgently at least in this?

Lisa sighed heavily, and tried not to think of her problem with Fowler soon gone. Fowler dead, or an exile returned home with Harry Archer's help, but anyhow, out of her life, now that there was absolutely nothing she could supply him with. He'd been generous about money—no doling it out, or even counting it—as if either money lay deep in his guilts, or he had more of it than anybody.

She was looking at herself in a last, satisfied appraisal when she saw Fowler swing his legs off the heart chair, then stand up unsteadily.

She went to him, and Fowler complained, "Damn, I can't feel my feet!"

"You've had them raised high—they're numbed, the blood hasn't had a chance to circulate."

He balanced himself, stooped over with one palm flat on the chair.

Lisa said, "If there's something I can do?"

Fowler said blackly, "Tell me where to swap an old-model heart for a new one."

He straightened up now, very slowly, as if he'd been deflated and air were being let in. He clenched and unclenched his fists, as if calculating his life force, then did some cautious calisthenics.

"The damn thing is," he said, "I feel good as ever. Not an ache anywhere, not sluggish a bit." He propelled his shoulders forward, to ease the stiffness, and then reversed the movement, snorting like a fighter. "It's just the bum ticker that fouls me up."

"You can learn to live with it," Lisa said. "Just do everything in moderation, get all the rest you can."

"Give a man a disability and watch the hecklers go at him," Fowler said unpleasantly. He scowled at Lisa. "Let's get on another topic."

Lisa pressed her lips together tightly. Soon she said with attempted casualness, "Did your business with Harry Archer go all right?"

"If it's a fishing expedition—" Fowler said, his eyes wise.

"Well, now, that exhausts that topic." Lisa furrowed her brow mockingly. "Let me see, what else can we talk about?"

Fowler laughed hoarsely. "You're clever, but not enough." His eyes fixed intently on her. "My bet is that you know every word that passed between Archer and me!"

Lisa's eyes were revealing. Fowler said, "To have a confidential talk in this house, you have to lock yourself in the john, open all the water faucets and use sign language."

Their eyes met, and Fowler nodded somberly. "The kick's over for me. I'm going home, back to my own kind."

Lisa flushed slightly. "Whatever that means."

"I've been a fish out of water here. Made an ass of myself at games I'm too old to play."

Lisa said, "Why not speak directly to God? You only mock Him when you attempt it through me."

Fowler frowned blankly. "Hun-h? What in hell did that say?"

Lisa held her tongue now, and Fowler said, as if it were deep and bitter in him, "That's another thing that's got me burned! It's like I just came off a boat, a greaseball in an English-speaking country. I need an interpreter around to tell me what's being said!"

Lisa said, "You really are full of complaints."

Fowler gestured angrily. "I've had as much of you and your smart crowd as I can take. You all talk and act like a bunch of sky people leaking down on the common herd." He shook his head disgustedly. "Sophisticates—brother, have I had a crotch-ful of them!"

Lisa smiled. "I read somewhere that there's an organic connection between a bad heart and distemper."

Fowler was silent now, as if wanting to dam the flow of bile in him, turn off the faucet of emotion. In a moment he said calmly, "One favor I ask of you, Lisa. For the balance of the time I'm around, talk to me in simple, everyday speech. No loaded sentences, no subtleties, no intellectual double talk." He managed a smile. "You want to call me a boob and a jerk, say it in the four letters, honest injun. I never mind insults I can understand."

Lisa laughed lightly, drawn now to his simplicity. "You're probably the only man ever who succeeded in making a whimsicality of an inferiority complex."

Fowler smiled thinly. "If I've got an inferiority complex, I developed it here in Mexico. I blame it on the Phi Beta Kappa expatriates I've met. I've been made to feel like the janitor at Harvard."

Lisa said, "And now you're going home. *To your own kind*. Full of contrition for your sins, past and present."

Fowler said, "You're up there leaking down on me. I don't know what the words mean, but I know I've been abused."

Lisa said, "The prodigal returns."

Fowler grinned. "Break it up even smaller than that."

"A *good* Catholic should know."

"I've been a *bad* Catholic." He stared thoughtfully at her. "Was *that* the sly dig before, when you cracked about me speaking directly to God?"

Lisa nodded. "You were in your way saying that you'd been in the muck, and you wanted now to cleanse yourself. The question now becomes, *who* insulted *who?*"

Fowler's brow knotted intensely, as if he was force-feeding Lisa's words to his brain. Lisa said, "You called it *games*, in a lovely euphemism. But how did your sudden penitent eye see me? As a playing partner, equally soiled, or as the muck itself?"

Fowler shook his head helplessly. "You talk English, but I hear it as Greek. I try my damnedest to make sense out of the words." He took her hand suddenly and cupped it in his own. He said acutely, "Look, I didn't mean to slap at your womanhood, if that's what this is all about. The words *penitent* and *muck* are your words—I didn't use them, or in any way mean to suggest them." He went on, fretfully now, "My quarrel is with myself—me, Fowler, exclusively, period. I've been a bad performer, out of my depth and element, and pretty damned absurd." He made a scribbling sign on his front automatically, unaware of his action. "I meant it only like that, in those limits. No God-thinking, no scolding myself for any sins, none of that."

Fowler sought earnestly to be believed. "God never bothered me, and in my mind I never conceded His jurisdiction over me. He's got His side of the street, and I've got mine. I'm a Catholic only because of my father."

Lisa said wryly, "I wonder how the voters in your home city would react to that speech." Fowler was watching her lips, as if reading them before hearing the words. Lisa smiled faintly. "A newspaper story I once read somewhere referred to you as, quote, a prominent Catholic layman, unquote."

His hand brushed impatiently. "You identify publicly with your church for practical political reasons. Do I have to tell you? You're judged by it, even by the non-Catholics. Get known as a freethinker, with no church affiliations, you couldn't get elected dog catcher. You've got every faith solidly against you. Catholic, Jew, Protestant."

Lisa smiled. "You rationalize so beautifully."

Fowler's eyes narrowed. "What's coming now?"

"I am sure that in your sublime depths, you are a very religious man. And *so* busily wrestling with the Devil, almost into your grave—like the true, classic Catholic." She shook her head. "Catholicism isn't so easily eradicated, or torn from the soul."

Fowler said slowly, "Is that what you really believe about me?"

"What I really believe, yes."

Fowler said in a small voice, "But even when I thought I was dying that other week, I didn't once think of God, or fall back into my faith. Lisa, I swear I didn't!"

Lisa regarded him critically. "Why do you make it such an issue of pride?"

"Why?" Fowler stumbled in his mind for an answer to it. "You deny something—why, Christ Almighty, you want done with it! It's aggravating to insist on something in the straightest language you know, and yet not get it across."

Lisa's brows raised skeptically, but she said nothing.

Fowler said, "I never asked you your faith." He essayed a smile. "While we're on the subject."

Lisa fluttered her lashes and said mockingly, "Pagan."

"Kidding aside!"

"Pagan," she repeated it seriously. "And even though you never thought to ask it, you *knew* it."

"Now what does that mean?"

"It's what attracted you to me. My outrageous paganism. Would it have been possible for you with an equally devout person?" She smiled archly. "And would it have been as much fun?"

Fowler wrested his eyes away. "I've had a dream of death every night since my attack. That's what decided me about going home—why I had Harry Archer fly out. Home is where I want to die, Lisa."

Lisa said softly, "You don't really owe me an explanation."

They joined looks again. Fowler said quietly, "You're disappointed. I didn't come through for you."

She said with tight self-control, "You've been more than generous."

"You wanted back to the Continent and your old life." There was the trace of a smile. "A salon for the elite, and you queen of the roost. That's why you picked up with me."

Lisa said candidly, "It's the life I'm best at, the only world I care about." She smiled to him. "I'm Eva's daughter. Eva, my wonderful mother."

She closed and opened her eyes, as a device against tears. "This has been my exile too, Ed. My own Devil's Island."

Fowler said with friendly banter, "If you only had the money."

Lisa made a face. "I detest being controlled by money and the rate of exchange. I loathe the sound of the word *pesos*, even more than I loathe Mexico."

Fowler said slowly and seriously now, "I feel that we're quits—even-Stephen with neither one of us in the other's debt. But I'll anyhow be your genie, make your wish come true."

Lisa stared with startled eyes. Fowler smiled. "I'm not

just making words. You'll have your villa in Cannes, maybe even that same one sold out from under you." The smile turned in, grew secretly. "You'll be big-league again—you won't have to keep open house for smart riffraff, like here."

She leaned forward tensely. "Why would you want to do it, Ed?"

He shrugged. "Damned if I know"—a smile flickered —"a bribe, maybe—so I'll get your vote. I'm a politician." He saw her eyes well up and he turned away embarrassedly. "Think I'll get dressed and join your party. I've had all the rest I can take."

She clung to his arm and impulsively kissed his cheek. "You're a more complex man than I thought, ever dreamed!"

He patted the top of her head, then stared somberly at her. "You puzzle me too, Lisa. As a woman, I mean—" He stopped self-consciously, censoring himself. He shrugged again, and said, almost to himself, "After two years, I know less about you than the first week."

Lisa crossed the floor to the closet. "What clothes would you like to wear?"

Fowler said, "Damn it, this is no slap at you, not meant to be unfriendly—" He stopped with the preamble, and pulled nervously at a slide-rack of suits.

Lisa said calmly, "I'll say it for you, Ed. Am I a woman, and if so, what kind of a woman?" She smiled. "Your mind is heavy with questions, so many questions—as a small boy puzzles over sex, how fantastic Sex is. You want to know: Have I ever really felt love for you, or even affection?" She shook her head regretfully. "The answer is no." She said quickly now, anticipating him, "Your question now is: How then could I have given myself to you, and as I did?"

"Without any feeling for me as a man, how could you?"

Her eyes on him were wide and calm. "I've been unable to answer it for myself, Ed." She smiled bleakly. "And lately I haven't wanted to."

Fowler stared dumbly, and Lisa said softly, "Questions, and questions. *Why* have there been other men, so many other men?"

Fowler said in a strangled voice, "*While* you were with me!"

She answered it as if in an improvisation. "It had to do with me, and not with you. You were not in it; it did not slight you in the least. Nor were you robbed of anything."

Fowler said, "It ground my guts. Knowing about it ground my guts."

"Then you should not have let yourself know about me."

Fowler said despondently, "It made me compete, try to somehow prove myself the best." He laughed harshly. "I had to try to win over men I didn't even know!"

Lisa spoke into the silence. "You viewed it only from your own ego, and that was too bad." She looked solemnly at him. "*Love*, or even affection—did you ever truly feel it for *me*?"

He thought about it desperately. "No, I suppose not."

Lisa pulled the sleeve of a blue silk suit from the rack. "Wear this one tonight. It makes you look slim and handsome."

Fowler eyed her silently, studying her dress, sniffing at her fragrance. His tone was curiously falsetto, like a

99

boy's. "Will it be so great, worth all the dressing up and perfume?"

Lisa said, "It will quickly become dreary, then nothing. She smiled at him now. "I do it both willingly, and helplessly."

Fowler was frowning with more things to say when she waved a hand in good-by and hurried out of the room.

14

Downstairs, Lisa stopped in the huge kitchen to look into the pots. The fixtures here gleamed aseptically; the refrigerator was a porcelain vault covering a whole wall. The equipment was a curious blending of old and new; mixed in with the fine copper pots and the stainless steel utensils were clay pots and bowls, iron pans, wooden spoons and beaters. The floor tiling was a soft blue, with a sunburst of violet and orange in the center.

Two native women in calico dresses did culinary chores and tended the steaming pots, under the austere supervision of Leona, the housekeeper.

As Lisa moved briskly around the kitchen the housekeeper retreated into corners of the room, as if seeking invisibility, a wall to hide behind. Her eyes were sad contemplating Lisa, like those of a deaf mute swelling inside with outcries she could not voice. Leona was of an age with Lisa, but wrinkled in the face, with drab gray hair combed as unstylishly as a wig and pulled into a librarian's knot in back.

At last, confronted by Lisa, the housekeeper said, "The *boeuf bourguignon* is without an ingredient. Laurel leaf was impossible to get."

"You remembered to marinate the beef squares in brandy?"

Leona nodded and quickly averted her eyes. The in-service role of gourmet chef on Sundays was galling to her. It reduced her, made her one with the native help.

Lisa said, "String beans *provençal*—I promised my guests. Just *one* clove of garlic. And *croissants*, Leona—you should have your mix ready."

Their eyes met now, as so seldom, in a reunion across the years. As girls, they'd sheltered commonly under one roof and sky, partners in a great secret; with the same young breasts and nubile beauty, with equal fears and follies and dreams, both with one eye for soaring with the robin, one eye dancing with this or that page of Elizabeth Barrett and Sappho.

Lisa wrested her eyes away, as from an unflattering mirror. *It's in the genes, something in the hormones*, she assured herself, seeking to combat the depression that these moments produced. *Age is biological, only that.*

She sought anodyne in the miraculous image of her mother. They'd been taken for sisters, even when Eva was over fifty. An odalisque nude to the harem veil on her lap, painted by George Koenig, hung famously in the Brussels

Museum—Eva had been so young of body at fifty-three! Another vision of her mother now stood in her mind: Eva at Maxim's, in cloth of gold, a fringed sheath creation by Worth that exposed rouged nipples—Eva dressed so, contributing risqué songs to an evening of nonprofessional entertainment. She'd watched and listened goggle-eyed, sensitive to the stares she got as Eva's surprisingly grown-up daughter. Eva had been a calendar fifty-five then, but biologically thirty.

Lisa's eyes swept the housekeeper critically. She saw the heavy ankles that rose beamlike to the hemline of the dress, the slattern figure, dripping breasts, the scrubbed cheeks.

Lisa snapped pettishly, "Time you wore a brassière that gives you support. And a girdle, Leona—for heaven's sake, give yourself some shape!"

Leona made no reply. Her face was void of expression and her eyes masked.

Lisa went on with it. "And a little lipstick—" Leona shook her head slightly, and Lisa shrilled, "It's your duty to others—you've no right looking as you do!"

Leona smiled secretively. "Who are you really concerned for, Lisa?"

Lisa flushed. "Don't be clever!"

Leona said calmly, "Instead of reviling me, you should congratulate yourself. Be thankful for how much better *you've* weathered."

Lisa stared at the housekeeper, then said bitterly, "Leona, I'm not a bit fooled. I know your sick, frantic soul —the queer way you think, what you're constantly up to with me." She looked steadily at the housekeeper. "Why do you stay on with me, and as a menial? Why do you punish yourself, and punish me? You're a linguist, you've a flair for writing. You could work as a translator for some publishing house."

Leona said flatly, "I'll leave the instant you dismiss me." Her eyes were mocking. "It's quite as simple as that to be permanently rid of me."

Lisa eyed her with hard dislike. Leona said evenly, "But you can't let go of anything, can you, Lisa? No clean sweep ever—you haven't the courage for it. You merely brush things into corners." Her voice sharpened slightly. "Like with Max."

Lisa flung her head back, as if shaking Leona's speech out of her ears. She looked around for the door, as if the kitchen and its layout were suddenly unfamiliar to her. She heard Leona speak behind her: "You're afraid of the new at the expense of the old. You want them both at once, nothing surrendered. Have you ever considered *why*, Lisa —really tried to understand it?"

On the threshold leading into the corridor, Lisa wheeled and said venomously, "You've a vile tongue, the grating voice of a disgusting old hag!" Her hands were shaking. "You'll never again know a kindness from me. *Or* be able to trap me into a conversation." She nodded violently to this last edict. "I command you never to speak to me. *About anything.*"

When Lisa was gone, Leona set her face muscles sternly and made big circles of her eyes, to keep the tears back. Soon she went about making the mix for the *croissants*. At a time of her chores, the remembrances commenced, as so many times through the long days and years. Memory revisited the sea shanty in Capri, the enchanted garret in Montmartre. She picked her way carefully, with her emotions firmly in check. As if it were all a riddle that required the calmest mind—if she was ever to find that answer in the ruins that would set her at peace.

15

In the corridor, Lisa stalled before an alcove of books, china dogs and knickknacks. She fooled with a vase of flowers on a taboret, rearranged the bouquet, while listening to the gabble of music and voices coming at her from the salons. She sighed heavily, as if already weary with the Sunday soirée. Soon, done with the bouquet, she dutifully went to show herself to her guests.

In the salons, there were bright hellos and her name called out. Then the stubby, bald man squatting near the hi-fi stood up. Lisa looked startled at the sight of him. Then, by mutual signs, he quit the salon to meet with Lisa in the deep corridor, out of earshot of the guests.

He kissed her cheek—a kiss that skimmed lightly, glancing off as if he'd put his lips to marble.

He said ingratiatingly, "You look beautiful, even younger than ever."

She said stiffly, "How did you know to find me here?"

"From the newspaper columns." He laughed. "You're still the celebrated hostess, even here in Mexico."

"The same self-assured Georgi Stroilov."

"*Not* Georgi Stroilov," he cautioned quickly. "I carry a Swiss passport issued to Karl Janoff."

Lisa said, "*Karl Janoff*. If it was only so easy to change a face!"

Janoff said reproachfully, "You haven't yet said that I am welcome!" He took her bare arm, rubbed it as if warming frozen fingers. "I am a lonely man, Lisa. This being cast out, an outcast—the terrible hungering for a friendly face!"

She stared silently at him for some moments. Stone-bald, she thought, where once the hair had been only thinning. And without a mustache now, the mustache ridiculously shaved off for disguise. She noted his suit, how the pants bagged with a porous look to the fabric, as if he'd been living in his clothes. She noted his shoes, the wear and neglect they showed, dirt-caked and bruised under a thin top-polish.

He seemed oddly shorter than he had in other years, was her thought. Did a man's height in some way relate to his other stature? She watched him flush under her scrutiny, self-consciously square his shoulders, stand stiffly and contract his diaphragm.

The same pig fat, she thought, shuddering with a private picture it formed for her. Put an apron on him and he's a squat, commonplace greengrocer.

An oddity of his recalled itself, and she spoke before she thought to censor the speech. "Do you still carry mints and shelled nuts in your vest pockets?"

Janoff gaped in surprise, and Lisa said quickly, "I didn't

mean it as a gibe. For some reason it popped into my mind."

Janoff read her face suspiciously, then showed two bulges in his vest. "Mints and peanuts"—he smiled—"some things are the same."

Lisa said, "You were a fool to come to Mexico."

"Where else but Mexico?" His eyes shadowed. "The fugitive's final sanctuary."

"Then the final graveyard," she said coldly. "And don't hope for anything so anesthetic or civilized as a bullet. This is a country of barbaric passions—they killed Trotsky with a paving block."

Janoff said calmly, "If I'm to die, I hope to be my own executioner." He showed the massive gold ring he wore. "There are certain pellets inside the shell." He laughed harshly. "The ring was once Stalin's gift to me. Have I never before shown it to you? It was given from a friend to a friend, with Stalin's hope that I would never have to resort to it."

Veins knobbed out at the sides of Janoff's temples. He said, as if obliged to explain, "A final flight to Mexico was inevitable, Lisa—I would not choose this peasant wilderness voluntarily! I was last in Spain, and then Argentina. In both countries, my visa was not renewed." He smiled grimly. "I found myself *persona non grata,* even to the Falange."

Lisa frowned, and Janoff said, "It is not so clear as it used to be. Red fascism and black fascism have made common cause." The tone dripped with irony now. "I found some sympathizers in satellite countries, only eager assassins in totalitarian countries. In Lisbon, Salazar's personal police deported me, after my life was twice attempted."

106

"You should then have asked for asylum in the United States."

He shook his head. "I am an anomaly—neither anti-communist nor democratic. This disqualifies me for political asylum in the United States. Since I am merely anti-Khrushchev, as Trotsky was anti-Stalin, I present no opportunity to their Central Intelligence."

Lisa put a hand to her brow. "The words make me sick. It's like an old headache returning." She said irritably, "Georgi, I don't want your confidences. Nor do I want you murdered here in my house!"

Janoff said softly, "Open house at Lisa's. Good companions and good talk—I've missed it!" He took her arm and squeezed it. "I'm still warmed by memories of Cannes and Biarritz—how many years ago was it?"

Lisa freed her arm. "Sentiment doesn't become you, Georgi. Your eyes become damp and more piglike."

He said in an unruffled voice, "*You* were sentimental once."

She said indifferently, "If that's how you *must* remember it."

Their eyes met in a long look. Janoff said, "I don't really remember it like that. It was mutually convenient, and that was all."

Lisa laughed. "If you're hoping I'll contradict you—well, I won't."

Janoff bowed. "You were always candid. A glowing virtue, rare in women."

There was an interval of silence, and then Lisa said harshly, "Stay on here and you're tempting the Fates. Choluca is a little Moscow of communism and Communists. They form an international colony, in liaison with the overstaffed Soviet Embassy in Mexico City. They intrigue, they form spy rings, they sing the *Internationale* and *Bandiera Rossa* in the village cafés with open bravado." She nodded surely. "They'll rival for the honor of murdering you, Georgi!"

Janoff said, "I'm fully aware of my danger here."

Lisa said, quickly now, "How stupid of me. You know, of course! These were *your* people until only recently." She laughed. "A good many of them probably selected and shipped here by you."

Janoff said, "My plan anyhow is to reside farther south, close to Yucatán." His manner was stiff and estranged now. "I'll only be a brief embarrassment. I'll be gone as soon as I can arrange for an automobile."

White patches formed under Lisa's eyes. She said resentfully, "How cheap of you to try to make me feel guilty!" She saw Janoff's shrug, and her voice blazed. "I have no interest in your quarrels—a plague on all your houses, I say! It was exciting once—it's a stupid bore to me today."

Janoff said with a goading smile, "You will survive, Lisa. No matter how the world spins, you will survive."

"Georgi, go to hell!"

Janoff watched her hurry swiftly up the corridor, away from the salons. He remained in the corridor for some minutes, as if not sure what direction to take.

16

She'd waited for Juan with morbid imaginings in their secret place, with pride the quickest casualty. The youth had calculated her true age, was Lisa's cold fear; his hands feeling the bark, counting each wrinkle one year. The total, much more than twice his own, had revolted him. He'd kept her waiting for that, out of malice and hurt manhood, in reprisal for having been seduced.

But she'd been wrong. He'd come finally with an apology for his lateness, speaking volubly in his native Spanish, and gesticulating. She'd understood only a few words; guessed it had to do absurdly with a marketing chore for his widowed mother, or some service for his invalid grandmother.

She'd stopped his speech by taking his hands.

She lay now in the ancient cave at the foot of the slope, with an ache in her spine from the uneven surface of the floor. And cold and clammy, as if the damp earth had seeped through the thin *petate,* was now seeping into her pores.

She sheltered against his chest, licked playfully at the salt taste of him, then scratched deep into the curve of his groin. He responded to it by raising over her, with his eyes searching into hers. When she shook her head he sank back to lie beside her.

Lisa said in English, "You're unwashed and smell like an animal."

Juan grinned foolishly. "*Sí, querida.*"

"Never discover soap, Juan. Smell foully, foul as sex is."

"*Sí, querida.*"

She looked at him from under her lashes. "Your sweetheart or wife someday should tie a pretty ribbon to you."

Juan smiled broadly, as if he understood the flattery by sense.

Lisa looked down to the tips of his toes. "You're long and lean, all bone and muscle."

Juan's eyes puzzled slightly, then when he guessed by her voice that it was another compliment, he said contentedly, "*Sí, querida.*"

"You're beautifully illiterate. You know nothing about politics or finance, or ordering a dinner, or home movies." Lisa shook her head warningly. "Don't improve, Juan. It will only make you sour."

Juan copied her head-shaking. "*No, querida, nunca,*" he promised.

Lisa ran a finger against the grain of his beard; circled the ascetic hollow of a cheek. "You're the son I aborted twice, the son I never bore. I'm Jocasta enjoying delicious incest with my son."

Juan frowned anxiously now, struck by her intensity. Lisa smiled sweetly. "Say, *sí querida,*" she said coaxingly.

Juan's face cleared. "*Sí, querida, sí.*"

She raised up on an elbow, to hover over him. "It's good to talk easily, without a pitting of minds. Oh, the blessed barrier of language!" She smiled down on him. "Do you wonder about me, or does it seem very simple to you?"

Juan smiled up at her, and Lisa said, "But you're so wrong, Juan. I'm with you only because you're a dumb beast, without mannerisms, rhetoric or conceits, just your sex."

Juan shook his head, as if it were becoming tiresome to him. Lisa said, "You make it vital, like an act of rape. No suckling at the breast, as if that was only incidental, the way it should be. But even so, it is all really nothing; the pleasure is too quick, too soon over. Now I'm self-disgusted and even more restless than before. And my back aches horribly and I'm catching cold."

She got to her feet and began to dress. "Besides, about now my guests will be wondering about me."

They dressed silently, back to back, in some estrangement now. When Juan, naked except for his cotton work shirt, bent over to put on a shoe, Lisa went sick over the image of a stallion it made for her. As they were about to leave, she remembered about the money. She pushed his protesting hands away and placed a sum of money in his shirt pocket. "For those other chores you neglected, *querida*, to perform this one."

Juan smiled brightly, then said, "*Mañana, querida?*"

Lisa said listlessly, "*Sí, mañana.*"

He went first, and she watched him go—his clothes open, his dragging shoelaces stirring up little combs of dust, and then soon the tail of his shirt flapping over his bottom.

She stifled the misery rising in her by sternly sealing off her thoughts, by closing every window and door in her mind, and turning off the lights.

17

The hum-mm of his plug-in electric shaver serenaded his ears as his own name said over and over, *Harreey-archer, Harreeyarcher, Harreeyarcher.* A smile stole into his face . . . gratitude for his name. It was short, easy on the tongue, explosive. It had a musical lilt, an insinuation of romance; too, it could be spat with bullet-swiftness, make cowards at once of susceptible opponents.

Harry Archer—he spat it scowlingly, tough-guy style, judging himself in the full mirror. He watched an imaginary foe quail, freeze into rigidity. He tried it sweetly now, his lips tasting the name like a fine brandy. At once intoxicated, he now conjured up that sprite who lived in the haunts of his fantasies. She danced nymph-like to the music of his name, hardly touching the ground.

He clicked the Off button of his shaver, stood taller on the balls of his feet, hoisted his shoulders hydraulically until the knobs showed hard and powerfully through the womanly casings of flesh.

Now soaring in his ego, he had fun speechifying in his mind. *I give you Harry Archer,* a molder of opinion, international salesman of good will and brotherly love, a man who . . . sold, sold, sold, New Jersey to runaway industry, capitalism to labor, democracy to Chile, plutocracy to the Dominican Republic, Irénée du Pont to Lemuel Goop . . . sold, sold, sold, Shipwreck Kelly, Cash-and-Carry Pyle, Batista to Cuba, revolution to Brazil, Cain to Abel, Abel to Cain, coals to Newcastle.

He winked victoriously into the mirror, then, offended by the pudgy face he saw, he tried firming it up. He jutted his jaw so the jowls receded into the column of neck, pulled down his upper lip to thin his snouting nose, deviled his weak eyes into the hard, steady gaze of the Cerebral Man.

The more familiar face, this, of Harry Archer, public relations counsel; the portrait pose now in the files of Underwood and Underwood, the morgues of the *New York Times*, AP and UP, *Time* Magazine, *United States News and World Report*, the Kiplinger Service, the *Manchester Guardian*, the *Daily Worker*, places, files, morgues, places; add Berlin, Beirut, Lisbon, Cairo, Rio de Janeiro.

His mind now assigned a title to the retouched portrait of himself. *Twentieth-Century Richelieu.* He laughed reminiscently in his throat. *Twentieth-Century Richelieu* had been the book title of the authorized biography of Harry Archer, written with sycophantry and biblical fervor by a minor employee of Harry Archer Associates.

He reached into his leather traveler's case for bay rum and talcum. While applying the toiletries, he mentally tallied up his possessions. He did this nervously and habitually, more than once a day, as if this were the narcotic that kept him in equilibrium, sure of himself.

Invisible fingers wrote on the slate of his mind a remarkably approximate penny count of his cash in banks; stocks, bonds and securities in vaults; and first mortgages. His inner eye pictured his real properties: the house in

New York's Murray Hill, that one in Southbury, Connecticut, that one in Chelsea, London, that one in the California desert.

He made words with his lips, talking to himself. *Got to sell* the white elephant in Chelsea. I try renovating it, putting new plumbing in, I'll never see a cent back. He nodded to this logic, then made a second resolve. Sell the Murray Hill house too. And right away, while it's a seller's market. Don't need a whole house, who in hell needs the upkeep!

His aplomb completely restored by the audit of his belongings, and feeling marvelous, Harry now refurbished that *one* scene nailed imperishably as a photograph on the wall of his mind: the hard times he'd known, the grinding poverty . . . invoked so he could revel more in his present affluence. And invoked, too, for subtler, less conscious purposes . . . that alibi to God, Conscience, Whomever, for the scruples he had given up in his zeal for himself.

He lay shivering on the hard leather sofa in the unheated office, with a light topcoat his only blanket. The window opening to an air shaft was painted black to eliminate the window washer. There was an upright L.C. Smith typewriter on an oak desk, and in the machine a short vignette written with sob appeal and an O. Henry snapper for a climax, addressed to Dear Mark. Dear Mark was Mark Hellinger, of the *New York Mirror*. A contribution to Hellinger, in exchange for column plugs for Sheila Connor, a night-club chanteuse, plugs for Marvo, of the adagio dance team of Marvo and Carlotta. He'd conceived the vignette, typed it up with his fingers stiff with cold—his payment for the overnight bed.

The legend on the pebbled-glass door of the office read:
MANNY SKLAR, PRESS AGENT.

He'd lain in a half-sleep, desperate for a smoke. Finally asleep, he'd dreamed of food, fat slices of white turkey meat, dripping, succulent dark meat, stuffing drenched with gravy, sweet potatoes richly glazed, hot rolls dripping butter. A dream cued by hunger pangs, and also the calendar. It was Thanksgiving Eve, 1931.

The scene obliterated, but the emotion of it still gripped him. In this aftermath now he was suddenly ravenously hungry, as if that hollow inside of more than a quarter-century ago still needed to be packed with turkeys, lobsters, steaks, pies. He lip-cursed Manny Sklar across the years: *the grubby, self-glutting* . . . For a flop and an occasional dollar, the bastard had me as a captive brain. I had the education, moron Manny had the brass. I did the work, Manny reaped the kudos and the bucks. The one time I signed my own name to a release to Winchell, Manny kicked me out.

Now cold currents of hatred welled up in him, and he vowed further retaliation against Manny.

As the wheel turns, Manny Sklar today was a desk-bound employee of Harry Archer Associates, an organization of three partners and twenty employees, lodged in a sparkling town house with a Florentine grillwork façade, in the fashionable East Sixties of New York City.

Archer had gotten into his tan silk gabardine slacks when his refurbished anger subsided. He softened toward Manny, saw him sentimentally now, as a souvenir of his own youth.

Manny was an object lesson anyhow, he told himself

now. Fang and claw, nobody hands you anything. The
year with Manny toughened me up, taught me the way of
the jungle. Who lives, and who falls dead. Manny was the
teacher; I owe him that much.

He visualized the current Manny. *The poor bugger's up
the creek anyhow.* Hasn't got a pot . . . still parks his
crate of a car a borough away, to make it harder for the
hoods from the finance company. Wife's got his testies, his
kids treat him like he's a boarder. If Manny was wise, he'd
go find a high building. But before that, cancel his insurance policy.

18

The six-o'clock chimes from the ornate mantel clock
brought the salon to sudden and curious quiet. The guests
in their little private oases in the room fell silent, leaving
colloquies and genuflections unfinished. They stood trancelike, stunned, as if in a sleep state, their eyes and heads nod-
ding with the chimes.

With the chimes over, they slowly rewound and reani-
mated, as if the count of six and the hovering echoes of it
had been an eternity of waiting in some deep, private obliv-

ion. And then, back to that more usual show of themselves, they drank faster than before.

The late sun lay flat on the big windows now: comet bursts of amethysts and emeralds and spears of burnished gold. The big chandeliers were lit now, mountainously aloof from the revelers, a crown of jewels seen tantalizingly through the haze and mists of cigarette smoke. All the guests had been drawn to the main salon, as if, with the omen of night, those strays in remote pasturing had wandered back to the herd.

Lisa surveyed the salon like a maître-de, blankly counting heads. She was reclad now, in a sheath of shimmering silver, looking gangling and elongated on high platform shoes and four-inch spikes of heels. She'd bathed and changed her scent since Juan, as if this rigorous hygiene, more than just an aftermath, was peculiarly bound up with and parcel to the assignation. Her face looked different, a new mask worn now; the mouth made smaller, into a Cupid's bow, so the sensuality was less, the high spirals of brows brought closer to the eye cave, and the merest trace of rouged-in color in her cheeks.

Her glance fixed on Fowler in a corner-of-the-room byplay with Donna Flores. Fowler stood very close to Donna's pregnancy, as if excited by it; his eyes sweating, his hands fondling where her arms and shoulders were naked.

Lisa saw Vito watching this intimacy with his wife. She guessed the impulses surging in Vito, and also that he was trying to suppress them. She saw the hand at his side clench and unclench, the eel-like slithering of muscles in his cheek.

She hurried over to him, to forestall his inevitable erup-

117

tion into violence. She linked arms with him, and firmly walked him away from the provocation.

Lisa flecked a kiss at the lobe of Vito's ear, in a calculated diversion. "How proprietary can you be?" she said lightly. "Can a man possess a woman more than you do Donna? Don't be so jealous of her fun." She smiled at him. "Male flattery is good for Donna right now. She'll have a happier pregnancy."

"The slob of a lecher," Vito said. "Doesn't he get enough of it at home?"

Lisa's smile fell only slightly. "My, what bad manners."

Vito flushed. "Lisa, I'm damned sorry." He kissed her cheek contritely.

Lisa changed the subject. "I've suddenly become unpopular. I've got food prepared for forty guests."

"There's an opening at the Galería Tajín," Vito said. He added grinningly, "When the canapes and drinks run out there, they'll come trooping in here. My advice is, stall the eats. Or you'll be serving all night."

Vito twisted so he could keep an eye on Fowler and Donna, but Lisa drew him away, to farther reaches of the salon.

"Help me select records," Lisa begged.

"Sure," Vito agreed reluctantly.

She drew him more into the partnership now. "Let's really do it up! Cliff Jackson, Jellyroll Morton, Fats Waller." She made her voice excited. "Bessie Smith singing 'Cemetery Blues,' and Louis Armstrong tootling 'Sugar Foot Strut.'"

Vito's eyes danced. "Where the hell did you get that great a record library?"

Lisa said distantly, "In my house in Cannes once, I could have shown you eighteen Cézannes."

Vito frowned, puzzling over the oddness of the reply. He was ready with a question about it, when she thrust a record album at him.

19

Over at the portable bar, Alec Taylor was the turbulent center of a group. On his usual tack, with the ancient record well-grooved and spoiling, a flaming address drawn from his crammed haversack of wares—said with hot eyes and spitting savagery, as umpty-times before in the bars, meeting halls, parlors of Beverly Hills, Carmel, New York City, Choluca. The subjects: Injustice, Liberty in Crisis, Man's Fate, Man's Hope, War and Peace.

Around Taylor were Susan, Hertzig, Harding, Archer: Susan vague-eyed, grasping for sense and meaning, held mainly by Taylor's fire; Hertzig amused, as if the phrases he heard were a code that deciphered into chuckling anecdotes in his private mind, to be retold other times, at other parties; Harding with the prophylactic stare of a social worker in a verminous tenement; Archer attentive, as if he knew a secret and tested formula for mining the gold of usable ideas from the everyday ore of talk, polemic, blather.

Well within earshot, but clever in his eavesdropping, sat Janoff, his face shielded from the group, and a bemused look fixed on it, as if Taylor's barbs hit keys that wrote Janoff's own personal story.

Taylor had so far drunk beyond sobriety and stupor both. He was articulate, remarkably clear in speech and mind. He spoke with a distant gaze, as if the small group before him were merely the foreground auditors of a limitless earth-mass of people. His voice was high and oratorical, leaping from an inner catapult straight to the ears of those listeners who stood solemnly and invisibly in the far corners of the world.

Taylor was saying, ". . . they bombed Milan, no quarter of mercy, so there were only skeletons of homes and rotting human flesh. One black-shawled witch of a grandmother was in the rubble filling a wicker basket, as if it was harvest time in a vegetable patch. Granny was insane and also sentimental. Or maybe the stuff in the basket represented trophies to her—flesh-proof of her amazing triumph. She'd after all outlasted and out-lucked her son, daughter-in-law and six grandchildren!"

Taylor squinted his eyes like an actor pretending to read off a legend written with letters almost lost in rust. "There was a sign twenty yards or so to the rear of the old lady. *Credere, obedere, combattere*, the sign said. The sign hung upside down now, like Fascism and Mussolini on the post in front of the gas station."

"So you were in the war, hip, hooray!" Harding said. "But it's been over now for how many years?"

Hertzig said, "Alec Taylor, the self-appointed Conscience of Man. He's really a priest, that's the funny joke. He's always preaching at people, trying to convince them and convert them."

"Crap on you, Victor!" Taylor said.

Archer sipped his drink. "Taylor was making some point—if you kibitzers would only shut up."

Susan said, "Alec, I'm sick!" She placed a hand over her breast. "You made it all so *vivid!*"

"And where was *God* in Milan during this horror?" Taylor went on. "In the cloisters of the Church of Santa María della Grazie, interposing for that treasure that was greater and more sacred than human life! Da Vinci's masterpiece, the *Last Supper*—a fresco protected with heavy wooden scaffolding and sandbags, to save it from the bombings. As it was saved, all praise to the Lord!" Taylor looked fixedly at Archer. "You were waiting for my point. Well?"

"War is hell"—Archer smiled thinly—"it's hardly an original point." He exchanged looks with Harding, and then made an elaborate business of fitting a cigarette to a silver holder.

Harding produced a lighter and held the flame out to Archer. He spoke over the fire. "Ask me, the atheist and holy man are twin brothers—from a motive point of view. God's ever uppermost in *both* their minds." He looked sidewise at Taylor. "Whenever I hear blasphemy, it plays back to me as prayer."

Taylor moved to confront Harding. "Nice, compact little aphorism," he said roughly. "Great for church advertising. But then, you've been trained to think shoddily in slogans."

Harding flashed a wry look to Susan. "I see I've been discussed." He pointed his next remarks at Archer and Hertzig, excluding Taylor. "Coming up is a blast against the sloganizing bastards of Madison Avenue. Somebody want to bet?"

"I'll settle for your summary of it." There was a hard glint in Taylor's eyes. "*Sloganizing bastards*—I couldn't improve on it."

Harding reddened. "Don't you ever inhibit yourself? *Think* before shooting off your mouth? At least for sociability's sake!"

"Never in certain company." Taylor's eyes mocked Harding.

Harding said, "I've seen dogs froth at the mouth. They can't help it, they're sick."

Hertzig sought to ease the mounting tension. "Taylor's a firebrand. He goes around losing friends and making enemies." He added grinningly, "He read Dale Carnegie's book, and like a Hollywood hack, he switched it around."

Taylor looked scornfully at the producer. "Hertzig's philosophy is love and please everybody. No pride about him, no damned spirit. Keep your foot in all the doors of the world, and never mind how many toes are crushed."

Hertzig tried to mask his hurt over the thrust. "Even where a man sensibly compromises. In his friendship, to keep a friend. In his marriage, to keep home and family together." He shook his head. "Not Alec Taylor."

Taylor glared angrily at Hertzig now; and then, made aware of Susan's eyes accusingly on him, he twisted to face her. He flushed and nodded slightly to her, in an unspoken admission of something; then he turned away.

Hertzig again attempted a lighter vein. "Taylor once

wrote an article denouncing his own film; he even called for a popular boycott of it." He made chuckling sounds. "This *after* pocketing fifty thousand dollars for the story."

"They'd phonied it up on me," Taylor said. "Some superpatriotic pressure group had gotten to the producer. They forced one of their no-talent loyals on him for a sneak rewrite. I wasn't consulted." Taylor made a face. "I puked when I saw the rough cut!"

Hertzig said banteringly, "The picture showed America as a going concern—a proposition that drives Alec wild." He stopped guiltily, in belated self-censorship. Taylor was looking at him with absolute disdain.

"My big mouth," Hertzig said sadly. "I just threw away what little chance I had of Alec doing a screenplay for me."

Taylor motioned at Hertzig and said generally, "The stateless Jacobowsky busy as always insuring his welcome. Grateful for any mean accommodations."

The producer paled, as if he was having a sick moment. Then his eyes trained defiantly on Taylor. "The accommodations here are fine," he said with his voice in tight leash. He added with plain meaning, "On this side of the Iron Curtain, the accommodations are simply great."

Taylor's mouth wreathed in disgust. "You've been sold an utter and outright lie, sucker!" He saw Susan's shocked reaction to his meanness, and nodded vigorously to her. "The bogey of persecution gets an automatic response from Hertzig. He doesn't bother sifting the truth—he merely reacts traumatically."

"It *is* the truth," Hertzig insisted heatedly. "And I wonder who of us is being subjective! Genocide against a minority religion and people. Hitler's own barbarisms, adopted by your great, shining humanists!"

"You not only *won't* get a screenplay from me," Taylor said blackly. "After this, you won't even get a hello!"

Hertzig smiled wanly and shrugged his shoulders. "In Cuba, Hemingway never invites me up his hill."

A silence lengthened, each person in the little group absorbed in himself, wary of the others. The white-coated native butler saw to the drinks quietly and impersonally, as if he were a machine servicing other machines.

In a while Archer observed musingly, "It's always remarkable to me how people work themselves into a tizzy over one issue or another—issues they have precious little understanding of; or anyhow, no power really to influence." He half-smiled and raised his glass to his lips. "It's a necessary food for the ego, I suppose. Man assuring his own importance."

Taylor looked critically at Archer. "Speaking of *points* —what exactly was yours?"

"No point. An observation merely." Archer saw Taylor's eyes hawklike on him and smiled thinly. "If I had a point, it's escaped me."

"Don't you mean you decided against making it? Thought better of it?"

"Hun-h?" Archer's brows elevated.

"It was a damned cynical point"—Taylor pursued it— "and you'd rather be regarded as a democratic fellow, tolerant of people. Isn't that your masquerade, Archer?"

Archer pressed his lips together. "I seem to be under attack." His eyes trained calmly on Taylor. "Suppose you make the point I neglected?"

"All right, I will." Taylor's tongue licked at his lower lip. "People are finally futile. They perform only as they are made to perform, with no say in their own destinies. Isn't that what you backed away from saying?"

Archer appealed to Harding. "Was I that philosophical, and on only three drinks?" He smiled thinly at Taylor now. "Sounds to me more like *your* special brand of theme."

"*Both* our themes," Taylor shot back. "We see people alike—sheeplike, quiescent and pathetic—but from different outlooks."

"Well, now"—Archer smiled broadly—"*Vive la différence.*" He studied Taylor curiously, as if marveling at the passion in the writer. "Can we drop it now?"

"I'm in the middle of it!" Taylor said coldly. "You must think of people as sheep, susceptible to any suggestion. For practical purposes. It's how you make your loot."

"Theme and *différence.*" Archer spoke into the silence. "What is our difference, Taylor?"

Taylor disdained the question, and Archer said, "You castigate them for being sheep. Am I putting it fairly? You explain the hell of their lives to them, how arid the pastures." The tone was subtly mocking now. "You show them a private stairway to heaven, herd them on it, whip them along in their climb if they falter." Archer smiled openly. "*Heaven,* whether they wish it or not. Whether they want a Messiah and Deliverance or not."

Taylor flushed slightly. "Very clever." A hand drew a circle around Archer and Harding. "You two package words as if you were classmates at the same university!"

Harding bore the thrust blithely, as if he'd decided to hold aloof, not let Taylor again bait him into argument.

Archer set his empty glass down on the bar. He took up

his new drink, revolved the glass in his hand reflectively. He set the drink down untasted, and turned to eye Taylor curiously.

"For a total stranger, you've been acting damned familiarly with me," Archer began levelly. "Have we by some chance met before, only I've forgotten?"

"I wondered when the prig in you would show," Taylor said.

Archer looked mildly exasperated, and Taylor said roughly, "I know you, Harry Archer. *Not* by close contamination, like now. You're famous, in a manner of speaking."

"I see." Archer kept his voice controlled. "Then you read about me, and formed a bias."

Taylor laughed unpleasantly. "I didn't read the puff articles."

"Of course not"—Archer smiled frostily—"You naturally read your own crusading press."

Taylor said, "You're pretty adept at in-fighting, hah, Archer."

"Is it a fight?"

"I don't bother you, hah?"

"Frankly, no."

Taylor turned away from Archer momentarily, and then turned back. "What does it take to get your back up, Big Man? Make you lose that fine self-control?"

Archer said coolly, "It would require a less obvious sort than you."

"Suppose I try anyhow." Taylor took a long swallow of his drink, then looked fully at Archer. "The firm of Sutter, Stevens and Archer once represented Japan's policies and interests *secretly*, without registering the fact as United

States law then required. The facts came out *after* Pearl Harbor, when we were already embroiled with Japan. Your firm was prosecuted and fined for it."

Archer said, "We paid the fine."

"No conscience about it?" Taylor's eyes touched Harding, Hertzig and Susan individually. "Your firm helped lull the American people, disarm our foreign policy. You could conceivably be called an accessory to the sneak attack on Pearl Harbor."

Archer said indifferently, "Are we done, or are you also going to rehash the asserted gift of a private plane to me by Perón and Evita?" A smile flickered. "I've also read your crusading press."

"Given a choice, I'd rather rehash your labor-relations stint in the long gone by. How Sutter, Stevens and Archer broke strikes by getting local politicians to rent you convicts at so much a head per diem. Bloody, murderous stuff, Archer, with whole towns sealed off in a news blackout."

Archer feigned a yawn. "My next biography, I might requisition your services." He smiled provokingly. "You remember almost as much as I've forgotten. And how pitiful that is."

"Pitiful?"

"What you've crammed your head with—and the fanatical recall!"

Taylor said, intensely now, "How do you live with it, Archer?"

Archer said stridently, in a first slip from self-control, "Shall we say, by keeping a pinup of your face in my memory. You were the spoilers, the traitors within, you and your kind. We were mainly the police."

Taylor's eyes glittered, and then, suddenly, he flung his drink.

The fluid splashed into Archer's face, ran down his collar and front. He first stared foolishly with wet eyes, then he ran blindly at Taylor, butting with his head and flailing his arms amateurishly. Taylor grabbed him, used his greater size to advantage, so Archer was a squirming, helpless bantam in the grasp of a heavyweight.

When Taylor threw Archer off, Harding and Hertzig intervened in the fight; they formed a wall between the belligerents.

Susan responded to a frantic sign from Hertzig; she took Taylor firmly in hand and led him away.

20

Janoff's eyes were intent on Taylor as the writer crossed the salon with Susan. He saw Taylor's face fully for the first time, noted the man's supple stride, the suggestion of hard flesh and muscular strength.

An American Communist in the arts, Janoff reflected—yet with the stern, unsmiling look and brute jaw of the official state poster of the workingman-in-arms hung in Czechoslovakia, Poland, Hungary, Rumania, Italy.

He picked over the bar tableau on which he had eavesdropped, selecting from the cross fire of dialogue all the speeches that had been Taylor's. He swiftly evaluated these, found the sum of the whole.

A party sheep—Janoff nodded with the derogation. Dedicated, parochial, mindless, submissive to the discipline of the black and the white. Sight fixed everlastingly on the twin god figures of Marx and Lenin, while dumbly and obediently shaping and reshaping his logic with the twists and turns of policy, the rise and fall and murder of personalities.

A feeling of depression filled Janoff and his eyes looked haunted now. The parochial Taylors were his jeopardy—the hourly and daily danger of atrocious assassination. This Taylor here, or another.

He imagined his murder—the brutality of it. His skull smashed with a heavy stone, as Leon Trotsky had been murdered in his Mexican exile.

He found a handkerchief and dried his sweated palms, and the eye of his self-pity now showed him in a derelict grave. He saw it in welling misery, and then another scene imposed over it. He was a young man in this, at the head of troops moving close behind the paladins of the October Revolution who were bearing the coffin of Nikolai Lenin to the mausoleum in Red Square. A war lord's burial, Byzantine and barbaric, with endless choral requiems and blowing incense, and then later, in the night-glow of torches and bonfires, a crowd numbering millions filing past the mausoleum to look upon the embalmed body.

A deification ever remembered—he'd fitted it into his own life plan, and into his fantasy. Wishing it for himself, in that late time of his own death—the homage and the magnificence, the sanctification and the legend. Wanting his brain too, like the Master's, removed and put in a specially constructed chest, to be cut into very thin slices for microscopic examination of genius.

He'd followed in Lenin's path all his life, hewing straight to the line; he'd studied, toiled, plotted, fought, decided, carefully seeded his mind so that what blossomed was the rich fruit of Lenin, as the Pope was the living voice of Jesus Christ.

Janoff's stare fixed lingeringly on Taylor, where he stood across the salon. Words and ideas he'd heard Taylor speak sounded once more in his mind. He retorted to some of them, gave the lie to others, exposing to Taylor those secret proofs he had. He saw Taylor blanch, stammer foolishly, go sick as revered ideas and idols toppled into the dust.

Janoff shook with laughter, a lunatic look in his eyes now, and a hand hard on his mouth as if stuffing the laughter back.

He looked over to Taylor more calmly, heady as he was with his imagined triumph over the parochial, idea-mouthing, slogan-parroting boob of an American Communist.

An American Communist—Janoff's face was wreathed with contempt, and he spat. As he'd spat at the same words all the long years before, and as others of the Politburo had spat too.

21

The Mexican bartender did incidental valet chores for Archer. He sopped up some of the wetness in Archer's clothes and on his shoes, using a bar towel, then smoothed the coat jacket with the flat of his hand. He averted his face from time to time, as if not to smile in Archer's view.

"The fellow's a paranoid!" Harding allied himself with Archer.

"I was a fool to let him get my goat." Archer got back into his jacket.

"Taylor had his hooks out for you on sight," Harding sympathized. "He was up on that soapbox, but quick."

"My cue to walk away." Archer smiled ruefully. "The only sound formula I know for fending with crackpots— leave them talking to themselves." He looked narrowly at Harding. "You, of course, recognized the propaganda tactic."

Harding frowned blankly, and Archer said it for himself, "Distortion and the big lie—reckless character assassination."

Harding said quickly, "Hell, I didn't for one minute think there was a word of truth in Taylor's tirade." A smile flickered. "I've had run-ins with the ilk myself."

"In your agency?"

"Brant, Bellows, Appleby and Harding. We've a radio and TV department." Harding frowned. "The situation was damned sensitive for a time. Sponsors kept pressuring us to clean out the reds, while the talent unions accused us of operating with a blacklist—stamping on people's civil rights and stuff. We were caught in between."

Archer grimaced sympathetically and made a sign to the bartender.

Hertzig showed unexpected interest. "So how did you resolve it, Harding?" Harding set his jaw, as if his first instinct was to withhold any answer. Hertzig smiled disarmingly. "I'm a collector of interesting but useless information."

"We didn't actually resolve or solve anything," Harding answered reluctantly. "We made decisions as we went along, on an individual-case basis."

"The performer or writer first cleared himself, so he could be acceptable to BBA&H." Hertzig smiled broadly. "Did I put the letters in the right order?"

"There was certain clearance machinery, sure." Harding scowled. "Mind you, *not* as part of the apparatus of the agency itself."

"A separate business entirely," Hertzig said. "Of course."

Harding squirmed uncomfortably. "Yes, I suppose it was a business for somebody." He squinted suspiciously at his interrogator. "You setting me up for something?"

Hertzig made a joke of it. "A financial investment, so I can produce a picture while I'm here. For under two hundred thousand dollars, I can shoot a wide-screen picture in Eastman color that will look like two million on the screen."

When the expected laugh didn't materialize, Hertzig said hopefully, "My idea is to also shoot a pilot for a half-hour television series along with the picture. *Two* for one, with not one extra penny cost!"

Harding shook his head. "My associates won't buy it. We were bitten once—blew ninety thousand dollars on a TV-pilot and trailers, produced for us by a fast-talking former radio packager whose only picture experience was photographing his children."

With hope quickly dissolved, Hertzig jested, "What if I deliver Alec Taylor as the script writer, would that change your mind?"

Harding laughed sourly. "I'll finance Taylor himself to the extent of a coffin, and out of my personal money."

"We'll split that tab." Archer crinkled a smile. "Don't hog the fun, Harding."

"Everybody hates Alec Taylor." Hertzig's tone was etched with regret.

"Everybody except *you*," Archer said wisely.

Hertzig nodded. "I can only respect and admire a writer. He makes us important. He takes our mean, insignificant little lives and raises them to literature."

"What hogwash!" Archer said.

"We're back with the oratory," Harding said.

"I've traveled with Taylor"—Hertzig smiled—"I grew new eyes and developed sharper senses in Alec's company. The world was suddenly exciting, to live in it was thrilling—I wanted never to die."

Harding raised mocking brows. "*Comrade* Taylor did all that for you!"

"Taylor is truly a writer," Hertzig said stubbornly. "The tragedy is, the Party ravished his talent." He looked to

Harding, and then to Archer. "I do not judge Taylor only by his politics. Politics are his neurosis, not the sum of him." There was a fleeting smile. "Who isn't in some things neurotic?"

"Write it all down as a love letter to Taylor," Archer said with disgust. "If your talk is any gauge of your talents as a producer—look out, investors!"

Hertzig smiled bleakly. "This is my day for impressing nobody."

Archer signaled the bartender to freshen his drink. He turned chummily to Harding. "Damn, has this been a day of listening to bull!" He motioned his glass at the room. "Is this the usual style of these soirees?"

"I'm a stranger here myself"—Harding grinned—"*and* an uninvited guest." He stared across the room at Susan, then made a sign to the bartender. When he saw Archer's glass tilted to him, he tapped his own against it.

"Cheers," Archer toasted.

"Cheers," Harding echoed.

Hertzig grinned foolishly, then made mumbling good-bys and drifted away.

Archer said, his eyes following Hertzig's retreat, "I've run into crap artists in my time!"

"Hertzig's pretty hard to take," Harding agreed.

"A moocher—do I know the kind! I wouldn't trust him any farther than I can throw him."

They drank silently, then had their glasses refilled. Harding tilted his drink at Archer, and again they touched glasses, smiling.

"I've watched you tense up a few times this last hour," Archer said. "And I've made a guess about what's bothering you. Wife trouble."

"*Ex*-wife trouble."

"Not the one here at the bar before?"

"The same. She divorced me here in Mexico."

"If that's so, what are you here for now?"

"I ask myself!"

"You're carrying a torch."

Harding drained his glass in a gulp. "Hell, we'd been married fifteen years." He smiled wanly. "After a stretch like that, you're at least sentimental."

"You mean jealous of your investment of time."

"Maybe that too." Harding stared at his companion. "You sound like you've been through it. Marriage and divorce."

Archer laughed shortly. "Your wife divorced *you*, what a break that was! I had to club mine into freeing me." He set his glass down hard. "Brother, did it cost—her lawyer really held me up!" He looked questioningly at Harding.

Harding shook his head. "She didn't ask for a cent. Even paid for her own divorce, as far as I know."

"You're either stone broke, or the lady hasn't got all her marbles." Archer stared across the room a while. "Her pairing off with Khrushchev over there—it mean anything?"

Harding mumbled an unintelligible reply.

"He's got an appeal," Archer said. "He's an underdog and martyred—how women go for that! I'd watch it, Harding."

"If that's the way it stacks"—Harding had trouble with his voice—"I've had it. Taylor can have her—no contest. I'm on the first plane back to New York."

Archer looked intently at his companion, and made

some judgment about him. "You'll stick around and make a fight of it, mister. You're a competitor, by your life's training." He smiled now and added coarsely, "Your balls won't be in it so much—you'll do it mainly to best Taylor."

Harding stared somberly across the salon. He said restlessly, in a low tone for his own ears, "Susan's a misfit here, out of her element." He heard Archer's laugh and turned to face him. "She hasn't the equipment or the savvy to dig weirdies of this breed. Hell, she's been a suburban matron most of her grown-up life."

"You might be surprised, Harding."

Harding frowned, and Archer said, "A woman is *two* people. It's the rare husband who gets to meet both of her while they're married."

"How the hell am I supposed to reply to that?" Harding said.

Archer laughed. "Cultivate the *other* woman you lived with but never actually met, if only out of curiosity. You might amaze yourself."

Harding searched Archer's face for some sign of a spoof. "You make it sound sinister," he said finally.

"You possibly won't find even a trace of your suburban matron." Archer's eyes were enjoying it. "You'll begin to think either you invented her, or Susan skillfully created the image for you, like an actress plays a role."

Harding said slowly, "What sort of woman does that make her out to be?"

"A wife," Archer said promptly.

"The dividing line, then, is between wife and woman? I mean, in that theory of yours about a woman being two people."

Archer nodded sagely.

"You're really soured on women and marriage," Harding accused. "You had it with a bitch, so all women look the same to you."

"I'm not *so* soured," Archer said, smiling. "The fact is, I'm taking a second plunge come Tuesday next. But on a more realistic level, more hard sense to it."

Harding said, "You make it sound like *business!*"

Archer laughed outright, in private enjoyment of something. He said, "Keep gawking at the stars and moon, you lose your pants and shirt." He clapped Harding on the shoulder. "How about another drink?"

22

Over at the hi-fi set, Vito Avedon wheeled to confront Taylor. "You sure got your ass in a sling with Archer. We could hear you all the way over here."

Taylor smiled, but his eyes were nervously on Lisa, assessing the extent of his fall from grace because of his rowdy behavior.

"So you fought at Anzio," Vito said incredulously.

"And in Spain in '38." Taylor could come to no conclusion about Lisa's true reaction to his manners. There was no clue in her face—her eyes on him were flat and un-

revealing. The door henceforth closed to him, he supposed
—the Sunday hospitality withdrawn, the free drinks and
dinners. *Another* blacklist added to his already impressive
collection.

"Two wars, huh?" Vito said, with his eyes hard on
Taylor.

"*One* War." Taylor turned his gaze fully on Vito now.
"One and the same enemy. We fought it in two phases,
with a long intermission between."

"You can make with the words," Vito said without
admiration.

"I'm an educated man," Taylor said wryly.

"Yeah, maybe even too much." Vito was frowning heavily, as if he had a bigger idea he knew no way to phrase.
He said finally, "Me, I lost out, there. I hung around the
streets and played pool when I should have been with the
books."

"You've got more equipment for living as a result."
Taylor winked covertly to Susan. "I can read Proust in
the French, Thomas Mann in German, and Cervantes in
Spanish. All with the help of a dictionary." He smiled to
Vito. "But I can't fix a leaky faucet, or wire a lamp, or
get a car going again when the gas line fouls up."

Vito looked closely at Taylor, to detect if he was being
derided. Then his upper lip raised and held over his teeth.
"The way you went at Archer, I figured at first he'd raped
your grandmother or something"—he waved a hand—
"but then Lisa here told me you'd never met Archer before
today!"

Taylor nodded. "No, I'd never actually met him before.
So what about it?"

Lisa, reading danger in the labored colloquy, said

lightly and artificially, "Alec was engaged in his favorite futility, tiffing with windmills."

"You butt out, Lisa," Vito said. His eyes fixed intensely on Taylor. "You meet and abuse a guy in one half-hour!"

"For what he represents." Taylor tried to smother his impatience. "Archer's on one side, and I'm on the other. Simple?"

"That tone of voice, knock it off!" Vito's eyes smoldered. "I'm not as stupid as you think!"

"You said it, I didn't."

Vito fixed his lip over his teeth again. "Hey, could you kill Archer?"

Taylor answered it obliquely, "If you don't kill Archers, you're dead."

"That's no answer."

"Isn't it?"

Taylor stared curiously at Vito, wondering what lay bottled below the mouth of the smoldering and inarticulate Italian. He planned his next speech to fit Vito's limits— frame a proposition the Italian could agree to loyally. "You take sides in life, Vito. Like you take sides in a war. Nobody's neutral, not really." His face drew into a somber look. "Can anyone take a neutral position in the war between good and evil?"

"You're conning me, Taylor. Good and evil! How's that about the Devil quoting Scriptures?" The old scar on his neck and cheek raised and welted. "I heard you sound off about God over there at the bar!"

Taylor looked sharply at Vito, and then at Lisa and Susan. He saw Lisa gesture secretly and frantically, her look to him forbidding any further exchange now that the true issue lay open.

"Taylor, you're a sonofabitch in your heart," Vito said. "If this weren't Lisa's house, I'd ram my fist down your throat." He wheeled, and quit the group.

"How cheap of you," Lisa scolded. "Being so patronizing with Vito.

"He's God-struck," Taylor said, his eyes following Vito across the salon.

"He has a right to be as devout as he pleases." Susan said it rebukingly.

"I'm caught between two lady floggers," Taylor said lightly.

Lisa spoke to Susan. "Alec feels rejected, so he overcompensates by bullying people. That's the key to his tantrums."

Taylor grinned raffishly at Lisa. "What qualifies a lowbrow like Avedon with you, other than his actress wife?"

Lisa said sharply, "And what qualifies you?"

"My two novels you keep prominently on your bookshelf." Taylor laughed, then put an arm around Lisa's waist and squeezed. "Very mad at me?"

"You're no better than a common saloon brawler." Lisa's smile forgave him. Her eyes fixed distantly now, on the group at the small bar. She watched Archer acting convivially with Harding. In her mind she went over the dialogue between Archer and Fowler she'd listened to earlier. She said almost inaudibly, "Archer repels me too. He's an oily little man—I mistrust little men."

"He's dirt," Taylor said incorrigibly. "A feeding jackal —some friend of man should shoot him."

Lisa prodded Taylor toward Susan. "Your escort is either very drunk or too sober—I can't decide which." She smiled sourly at Susan. "I charge you with responsibility for Alec. At least until Archer has left." Her eyes now found Janoff, and she said restlessly, "I'm sick to death of political minds and political talk!"

She was startled to hear Taylor's voice close to her ear. "He's been here an hour, but hasn't mingled. Or even been introduced around. He just sits there in that fat Buddha pose. Who is he, Lisa?"

"A man I once knew." Lisa averted her eyes. "He was passing through Choluca and dropped in unexpectedly." Her hand fluttered nervously. "I'm afraid I didn't make him feel welcome. I can't understand why he's still here."

"You're an attraction men find hard to resist." Taylor looked sharply at Lisa, his curiosity whetted by her obvious disquiet. "He has a name, hasn't he?"

"Why, yes." *Georgi Stroilov* was in her mouth, but she caught herself in time. "Karl Janoff."

"Janoff?" Taylor repeated the name frowningly. "German, or is it Russian?"

"You're not really going to make me supply a pedigree?" Lisa affected a careless tone.

"Never deny a writer biographic material." Taylor's eyes were away, hard on Janoff. "It defeats our craft—the well dries up. Damn, what's the mystery to your unwelcome guest?"

"He's an old flame, and for that, a dreary bore." Lisa frowned forbiddingly. "I have only unpleasant memories of him, and I don't want him back in my life, even for one evening."

"The speech is very out of character for you." Taylor sought to see into her eyes.

"Alec, you're deliberately provoking me!"

"You're the provocative one in this," Taylor persisted. "You keep dissembling, and not as artfully as I would expect." He motioned in Janoff's direction. "That bald chap there is an embarrassment to you, all right, but not for the reason you gave." He smiled now, and winked privately for Lisa. "Even twenty ex-lovers in a room wouldn't bother you, or for one minute cramp your style." He saw her underlip draw and whiten in quiet anger. "All right then, *taboo*—I'll get off it."

Lisa edged away, requisitioned a new smile from her stocks, then crossed the salon trippingly to mingle with another set of people.

23

With Lisa gone, Taylor kept staring across the room at Janoff. He noted the generally shabby look of the man, the forbidding reserve of manner, and the posture of him as he sat—stiffly erect with the straight spine characteristic of the military, his hands palms-down and flat on either knee. The impassive face and expressionless eyes intrigued Taylor last and most. He had a nagging sense of having seen the face and look before. It had a *value* that belied the superficially shabby look, as if its owner was somebody of substance, a force in his own milieu, and the quick, outer impression he gave was false, intentional or not.

Taylor closed his eyes, as if instinctively seeking the dark, better to cull through those photographs stocked away in memory. He stopped on a few, all personages once in his ken, opening his eyes briefly to compare each separately with the face across the salon. Then finally, he stayed in rapt study of *one*, with his heart hammering and his blood cold. This photograph in his memory stock was younger than the man he was observing, twenty years younger, not so corpulent, with a shock of wool-hair and a black mustache. The resemblance, for what there was, lay in the *value* of the face, its stone look and veiled eyes.

Gómez, Rotha—Taylor shook his head at once to the improbability of it. He'd been struck by faces before, how many hundred times? As if eternally seeking to pin that face haunting his memory to some flesh form in present sight, however mistakenly. And always the names *Gómez, Rotha,* whispering in his brain. Gomez alias Rotha, a specter of his youth.

He stared across at Janoff doubtfully now. He made a last test of identity: he altered the photograph in his memory so that the mustache was gone, and the hair cropped close and dyed a tomato-red. Then he compared this with Janoff's face.

In a while, he stopped his game. It played hob with his nerves; he well knew it as a symptom of an old sickness.

He wanted a drink badly now, and returned to the bar. Oblivious to Susan, he left her behind him, standing alone. The bar was deserted, and then Hertzig came to stand with him.

143

Hertzig said tentatively, in a small voice, "Alec, I didn't mean to quarrel with you."

"Victor, you really hung yourself with me!"

"I've got a good and bad opinion of you." Hertzig half-smiled. "I try to understand you."

"Victor, drop dead." Taylor twisted away from Hertzig and downed his drink, his eyes again fixed hypnotically on Janoff. He reached out blindly and drew Hertzig to him now.

"That man there," Taylor said tensely, motioning a hand. "*Karl Janoff*, according to Lisa. You collect faces—you've wandered the world. Know him?"

Hertzig was slow in replying. He said finally, "It's a face you meet in the lobby of any cheap hotel. In Times Square, in Munich." He laughed scratchily. "He's an importer of heavy machinery, he buys and sells scrap metal."

Taylor looked sharply at Hertzig. "What the hell kind of stupid reply is that?"

"Ask impossible questions, you get stupid answers."

Taylor said, "Victor, I know you well enough to smell an evasion!"

Hertzig shifted uncomfortably, and Taylor grasped his arm. "You *do* know him," he said fiercely now.

Hertzig freed his arm. "Alec, I've seen you crazy. But never like today."

"Victor, who is he!"

Hertzig said slowly and reluctantly, "What a joke that *I* have to identify a comrade for you—"

Taylor said suddenly, "Georgi Stroilov, of course!" His face filled with absolute loathing. "I had an immediate revulsion for him, deep in my guts. As if I knew the bas-

144

tard at once, but subconsciously." He turned angrily to Hertzig now. "You called him a comrade of mine. Wash your mouth!"

Hertzig reached out and grasped a whiskey bottle. "Sure." He looked somberly at Taylor, and then over to Janoff. "You stand as twin jaws of a vise, with humanity crushed in between."

Taylor stared, struck by the unexpected remark. He said scowlingly, "What . . . was that hunk of philosophy?"

Victor poured two drinks from the bottle. He smiled at Taylor, motioning at Janoff. "Don't let me distract you from the fullest enjoyment of your hatred."

24

Susan pressed thumbs to the sides of her temples. "It's been like roman candles going off in my head. No stop to it for hours!"

"It did get a little wild," Taylor agreed.

They were alone in the second salon, beside the lighted glass case with the small jaguar gods in colored jadeite.

Taylor's tongue licked dryly at his lower lip. His cheeks were ashen, the flesh under his eyes made little mounds. "Damn, I can use a drink," he said.

"You've drunk too much already. It's made you *inhuman*." Susan smiled involuntarily over the word she'd used. "God, my head!" Her thumbs made little revolutions, kneading the flesh.

"Get you some aspirin?"

"No, I'll be all right." Her mouth furrowed at the corners. "I used to react like this in college lecture rooms. Headachy, as if I'd been drugged."

"You're being very unsubtle," Taylor said.

"You were being purposely offensive with everybody," she said. "You made no attempt at a rational exchange of ideas with anybody."

"You don't exchange ideas with scum."

"Alec, please, no more tantrums today!"

"Tantrums was Lisa's word. Don't be so easily influenced!"

"Oh, God," Susan said. "You're even unfriendly toward me." Taylor put a hand on her shoulder. "Sorry," he said. "I am wound up and jumpy, I guess. "I slept damned poorly last night, woke up in the dumps."

"You've been drinking steadily for days. "I've never before seen you drink so compulsively!"

"I've had a sense of overhanging doom all week. All sorts of wacky imaginings. Walls closing in, ceilings zooming down to flatten me out." He tried to smile. "My active inner life!"

"Alec, it's what drinking does! Alcohol's a depressant."

"Like I felt during those last months in Hollywood—" There was a haunted look, and his breathing was suddenly difficult. "Obstacles in my path that I couldn't by-pass. And *jeopardy*—everything and everybody threatening me, plotting to get me." He swayed unsteadily and bumped against the lighted display case. "My food poisoned, and the drinking water. Every car in the street aimed at me like a projectile." He straightened up and the display case corrected its dangerous tilt. He closed and opened his eyes into staring circles. "I'd dream nights about gas blowing at me through the steam radiators. I'd get out of bed and turn off the valves!"

Susan retreated a step involuntarily. A shudder ran through Taylor and then his eyes sought her out. He saw her frightened look and smiled bleakly and self-consciously. "You're now one of the privileged few ever to get a peek into my case book."

Susan said tensely, "You're being the writer again, saying anything that comes into your head!"

"All sounds improbable, sure," Taylor said. He stared contemplatively at her. "Want to hear what finally snapped me out of the funk that other time?" He didn't wait for her reply. "I was in L.A. one afternoon, walking along Fifth and Main. My car'd broken down, the rear axle, and I had an hour to kill waiting for it to be repaired. It was raining cats and dogs, a high wind, heavy thunder. Then it suddenly got me—that feeling of overhanging doom. With physiological symptoms this time. My legs went dead, there was a paralysis right up to my thighs. I couldn't walk, move one step." His hand cupped his jaw. "And here, a kind of lockjaw. I couldn't speak or make a sound. I stood transfixed, like stone, with an omen of death all through me, sure I was about to die. This was *it*, that climax I'd been dreading for weeks and months." He stopped and made short, growling sounds in his throat.

She took his arm, with the horror of his plight mirrored in her look. He wrenched his arm away and pushed her from him. He said, "A lightning bolt in the sky. Low, right down to the rooftops. Then a cornice fell from a building, zoomed down to the sidewalk." He laughed suddenly, a laugh that climbed in pitch as the congestion in his throat dissolved.

Susan watched him with an odd quiet, as if seeing him for the first time, and filing this in her mind as a postscript to those other conclusions she had reached about him. She said, "You're attracting attention. Alec, please!"

Taylor's laugh cut off. He eyed her solemnly for a moment, then said, "The cornice killed a man who'd just passed me on the street where I'd stopped. It crushed his skull, almost cut him in two!"

Susan gasped and put a hand over her heart.

Taylor plunged his hands deep into his pockets. He stooped momentarily to peer at the exhibits in the lighted case. When he turned back to her, he was more normally himself. The disturbed look was gone. He said conversationally, "I'm not mystically inclined, so I never tried really to interpret it, or value it. But I was fine from then on, I felt fine. The symptoms gone, the fears gone, some of my optimism back."

Susan said. "It must have been a horrible experience!"

Taylor said, "A week or so later, I became curious about the victim. The newspaper accounts had provided only slight information about him. His name was Charley Connors, he was fortyish, he had a wife and son, he was a securities salesman, and that was all.

"I went to see Mrs. Connors, had a talk with her. She

told me about her late husband, showed me snapshots of him." Susan's eyes were raptly on him and Taylor smiled. "He'd been a big fellow, with close-cropped hair, and a dent here high on the nose, like I've got a dent. He'd been a securities salesman, but he'd also done a pile of writing. Poetry, a couple of unproduced plays, one or two unsold novels. And not an indigenous Californian—Charley'd emigrated from Illinois, had been born and raised in Chicago. He'd graduated the University of Wisconsin, class of '34. His death was a blow, the boy missed his father— Mrs. Connors was back with her steno pad, trying to look delectably young for the office wolves."

Susan said in a small, awed voice, "You've described yourself!"

"I described Charley Connors," Taylor said. "No dumbing it up, no editing it to make a better story. Susan, I've given you the facts, *exactly* as I researched them."

Susan's eyes were round and incredulous. "But a man like yourself, with *your* face! Born and reared in Chicago, as you were; and like you, a graduate of the University of Wisconsin!"

"Class of '34," Taylor said. "I'm class of '36."

"It all sounds preposterous." Susan laughed uneasily. "Alec, you *know* you made it all up!"

"No. I give you my word. Want proof, I can give it to you. Any time. I've got news clips in my luggage."

Susan looked baffled. "Supposing it *did* happen; that you have been truthful. Then this Charley Connors, a man like you, was a sacrifice for you. That's how you really think about it!"

"Sometimes, perhaps." Taylor smiled wryly. "In weak-minded moments, when I must believe that I'm finally

149

indestructible, and ego alone isn't assurance enough." He reached to touch her. "Look, I don't tell the story often." He laughed shortly. "People would organize to have me put away." His fingers pressed into her arm. "It leaks out of me when I've got the shakes, like today. You've heard it, now forget it." His eyes were on her, waiting for her to nod.

A servant carrying a tray of used glasses passed Taylor. He stopped the man and poured the leftover liquid from several glasses into one glass.

"The drink's any good, we'll bottle and advertise it." He grinned at Susan.

He downed the drink, making a face over the taste, then sighted the group at the bar through the bottom of the glass. "The vultures are picking me over," Taylor announced. "I can almost lip-read your ex proclaiming that my mother was a whore."

"You did your best to make him dislike you."

Taylor grinned. "He would anyhow, things being what they are." He looked critically at Susan. "What hope did he bring all the way from Madison Avenue?"

"A reconciliation."

"What are his chances?"

"What do you think!"

"Old habits cling. You've had His and Hers towels and pillowcases, for how long was it?"

Susan flushed. "If you must make fun of me."

"But he's won reconciliations before. You told me so yourself."

She looked levelly at him. "I'm not the woman I was those other times."

Taylor half-smiled. "That knocks over a pet Freudianism. That patterns repeat to the end of life. That you can rationalize a susceptibility, but never evict it."

"Alec, please stop being clever."

Taylor smiled. "I could be bucking for a compliment."

She squinted her eyes, and Taylor said, "That I'm your immunity to any habit-reflex over Harding." He looked narrowly at her. "But I'm not, huh?"

She looked fully at him. "Does it really worry you so much?"

He stared at her, then said carefully, "You don't make love to a woman just to pass the time." His smile flickered. "There's checkers, and bird watching."

She said, "You're being glib. Using words to cover your lack of any real feeling."

"The snide remark that emasculates." Taylor shook his head at her reproachfully. "I had you tabbed as another kind of woman utterly."

Susan said, "You confuse me. I don't know when to believe you."

He tipped her chin so their eyes met. "Proof positive that your ex-husband still wields impressive power. He's got us quarreling, merely by his presence. A wedge suddenly between us wide enough to accommodate a team of mules."

Her eyes flashed angrily. "I didn't in any way welcome or encourage him. I told him flatly he was wasting his time."

Taylor smiled now, as if relieved and reassured. "Then what's got me so in the doghouse? I mean, aside from my foul manners and stuff."

"Your lack of candor with me," Susan said. "When I've been candid with you, and without any reservation."

Taylor said slowly, "Candor is a job of undoing knots. Knots just won't undo for some people."

"You none the less had that obligation to me," Susan said. "As much *truth* as I'd given you."

"Don't sound so god-awful bourgeois!"

"And what if I am bourgeois? If that is the basic me."

"Then you should have bargained that way from the start. Given only as you got. Made certain of the *quid pro quo*." His eyes mocked at her now. "Weighed the diamond for the carats—gotten a rating sheet on your suitor before jumping into the sack."

She said with surprising calm, "My, how you thrash."

He stared moodily at her. "Match living scars with somebody, romance cops a walk. The atmosphere gets too morbid, as sterile as a hospital room." He saw her smile. "I know! I'm still being glib—using words as a cover-up."

"Well, aren't you?"

"Look, I've told you things about myself. It's been a damned talkathon for weeks. Whatever I held back was not done to snare you, or deceive you."

"Then why did you? Hold things back, I mean."

His eyes clouded. "I've tried to put part of my life out of my mind. Not think about it."

Susan said, "Alec, I want to know about your marriage, your family."

He said slowly, "I'd need more reasons than just your curiosity, or *quid pro quo*." He met her eyes, then smiled grimly. "All right, I'll open the closet so you can stare at skeletons. And I predict that we'll both be sorry I did!" He looked about restlessly. "But somewhere more privately—let's take a walk somewhere. And I'll need a drink in my hand."

25

The easterly wing of the villa tipped toward the village proper. It was a square, severe and compact; it sat low in a hollow, with no visible bottom definition, as if risen from the bowels of the earth. Its ground level here, actually a basement, was a bulking cubism of somber gray and pebbled mortar. On these two sides of it no windows showed to passers-by—its mausoleum-like look made even truer and more remarkable by the contrasting blue-and-white-tiled elegance of the other architecture.

There was a separate outside approach in the back, an uneven stone path rimmed with bare-limbed willow trees that went up and then down, terminating before a heavy, studded Spanish door with an enormous, unserviceable keyhole.

Interior access from the main level to these essentially servants' quarters was through sudden corridors that seemed unfunctional and baffling, and then finally a steep descent down primitively crafted stone stairs. The uninitiate in the Villa de la Soledad found the basement only by exploration.

Taylor took Susan's hand and guided her down the stone steps. As they got lower, the basement gloom painted their faces blue.

"God, it's like descending into a crypt!" Susan shuddered. "Did we *have* to come down here?"

He squeezed her hand reassuringly. "There's a door somewhere leading to the outdoors."

She was looking at him questioningly. "I poke around in odd places," Taylor explained. He motioned. "There are three or four rooms, and a kitchen. The help have their own community. If Lisa ever took census, she'd find three for every one in her hire. And that doesn't include babies and livestock."

"A place to live," Susan said.

"Live in their own custom, as crude as they want it, and damn the sleek fat-cat *norteamericanos.*" He pulled her in his path. "Come peek."

The opening to the native kitchen was arched like the mouth of a tunnel. Taylor and Susan looked in, not entering.

The kitchen was the central room, with alcove bedrooms off it—all of it at once exposed like a stage set. The kitchen walls were mud-red, the concrete rude and unfinished, with innumberable crannies and gashes on the surfaces. Heavy wooden beams supported the ceilings. One corner of the kitchen had been made into a home chapel; there was a figure of the Virgin Mary in a portable niche embellished with the *zempasuchil*—the marigold, the flower of the dead—and tortillas, ears of corn, fruits. A second niche had an agonized Christus with realistic bleeding hands and feet; arranged around its narrow ledge were photographs of the family dead. Votive candles were the only light in the room—they made little pools of golden glow, threw mezzotinted figures into odd dances on the mud-red walls.

A six-foot wreath of marigolds stood against a wall, with hanging bags of dried chili and ropes of garlic cloves above it. There was a long table with baskets of food and pastries, the frames of the baskets decorated, all packed and ready for the trek to the cemetery—the dead there to partake of the essence of the offerings, leaving the substance to be eaten at an appropriate time by the mourners.

On a wooden pole with a crossbar were twin purple macaws, surveying the kitchen and the humans in it with nervous eyes and beaks, their mouths working rapidly and silently as if first deciding and rehearsing the torrential jabber they would later emit.

There were three women and an infant under the eyes of the macaws. The women represented three generations —two of them garbed in heavy black, and the third, a luminous beauty with flirtatious eyes and a flower in her hair, wearing a decorous black *rebozo* that could not quite hide the frills of lace of the pretty dress underneath. The women toiled at separate tasks, working rapidly and urgently as if there were a great ticking clock and an impatient overseer in the room. They were chanting religious hymns in chorus, in broken phrasings, very low, and with scarcely a melody—unaware of each other or the choral effect, as they were even unaware of the act itself.

The infant sat on the floor, round and fat below a smallish head—in the shape of a gourd; his hand was balled around a death's-head of sugar which he kept trying futilely to bring to his mouth.

They stood barely inside the basement now, before the heavy, studded door that opened to the outdoors. The door was ajar, with the bare willow trees narrowly framed in it. Susan was looking expectantly at him, and Taylor said, "You'll hear it with a woman's ears—conclude about me that I'm an insensitive brute." He looked lingeringly at her and smiled gloomily. *"Fini, la commedia è finita. We'll be done with each other, right away and at once."*

She moved closer to him, touched by his distress. He seized her in a crush of arms, his fists balled so hard she felt the mold of them where they pressed into her flesh.

She pulled free, sucking air as if her lungs had emptied. Then Taylor began: "I was married for fourteen years. One marriage, one wife. Helga Kohler, a girl from White Fish, Montana, stranded in Hollywood, friendless and penniless. She'd fled a brute bastard of a German father, a logger for the state lumber mill. She was in Hollywood for the reasons fifty thousand other girls were there. Fan magazines she'd read, Clark Gable and Jimmy Stewart and the male-image worship. And the hope that somehow, somewhere, she'd be noticed, a talent scout would pop his eyes over her. She had her face, measurements and pedigree filed with casting agencies; she moved to a new address whenever the rent was so much in arrears."

Taylor lit a cigarette and puffed it hungrily. He spoke from behind a wall of smoke. "I met Helga through a cab driver who made a side dollar working as a pimp. I was on my first screenplay; I'd been brought out to dramatize a novel of mine Columbia Pictures had bought. I was frightened stiff and nervous, totally inexperienced in the craft and writing by rote. I'd watch movies all day for orientation, and then write at night." He shook his head slightly. "I'm not digressing. What I'm trying to do is explain *how* I came to get involved with that pimping cab driver."

Susan said, "You were full of insecurities, and it expressed itself sexually."

"That analyzes it, or does it really?" Taylor tried to smile. "Look, my marriage went to hell a long time ago. It's dead with history."

Her mouth set firmly. "I've told you about Richard and myself, even more that I wanted to. You pumped me constantly, drew every tiny detail from me."

"But only for the story, I'm a writer, and for that a voyeur. I didn't probe or pry in order to judge you, make any male decision about you."

Susan said, "You're not really going to make me *drag* the story from you!"

Taylor chewed at his underlip. "Fade back in on the pimping cabbie. Did he know an acrobatic whore who would shore up the morale of an insecure screen writer? He fixed it for me to meet Helga—and soon enough, we were off to Tijuana in a rented convertible for a week end of sex." He laughed shortly. "I even remember the economics of it. Twenty-five for the cabbie, and one hundred clear for Helga."

"A whore should be something faceless, no individuality, a body only and animal lust, or the clever pretense of it. But I was romantic, even saddled with idealisms about my mother, the milk-giving godliness of the female body, et cetera and so forth." He smiled cloudily. "I was an esthete, imagine, and more likely than not seventy-five per cent unconscious nance at that stage. Anyhow, the fact that I'd bought Helga's time and services was forgotten before we were ten miles along the Pacific Coast Highway. We had the top down; it was a fine, clear day, with a fireball of a sun. In San Diego I bought her stockings, a silk dress to replace the rag she wore, and a cheap dyed-rabbit-fur stole I'd watched her eyes adore. We drove to Tijuana holding hands across the car seat."

Taylor lit two cigarettes. When Susan refused the one he offered her, he threw it to the ground and stamped it out. "Give me a sign, and I'll stop," he said. "It's becoming a tender reminiscence. If I were a girl at all involved with the fellow telling it, I'd be steaming with jealousy by now."

Susan said, "You tell it as if you've needed to. And for a long time."

Taylor grimaced. "Grow a beard and hang out a shingle. Where was I?"

"In Tijuana."

"In Tijuana it really became a ridiculous boy-girl idyll. We went to the jai alai games, shot rolls of film, spent nights in tourist traps, filled suitcases with trinkets. The first night, there was no roll in the hay, as such. We had champagne in an ice cooler in our room, soft lights, sweet music. We jabbered endlessly, swapped histories and philosophies." Taylor made a face. "I *wooed* her, and funny thing, on that level, Helga was hard to push over."

Taylor paused and then said, "I'm really giving it the full treatment, and I still insist, you're a damn fool to endure it."

"You're telling it the only way you can." She smiled. "Honestly, I don't mind a bit."

"Writers are congenital fakers." Taylor returned her smile. "We magnify trivia, give it a high gloss. Our worry is, somebody might confuse us with the butcher and the barber—decide about us that we're not so much, common-place as anybody. You're a sucker if you accept as literal truth *my* version of anything pertaining to me."

He waited for some comment from her. When none came, he resumed. "Dissolve on the week end. Came Monday, I got back into the studio whirl, didn't think at all about Helga for months. Oh, yes, one thing: I never paid her that one hundred. It either slipped my mind, or I was too sensitive to offer it. Anyhow, she never requested the money, then or later."

Taylor was momentarily silent, as if condensing a volume in his mind. "I finally got that first screenplay done. It wasn't up to expectations; was, in fact, pretty amateurish —the studio had to assign two other writers to fix it and polish it. But I wasn't sent packing—my option was picked up. I was given a three-year contract." He laughed softly. "It wasn't a case of abiding faith in me. I had an agent with a knack for cajolery and a genius for blackmail."

"I'll get to how I came to marry Helga now. Some months after the affair in Tijuana, I became engaged to a girl, Myra Bentley, the well-reared, pampered, only daughter of a prosperous Beverly Hills realtor and political Republican. Myra was only twenty, but she already owned a mink coat and a flashy sports roadster. I'd been formally introduced to her at a party, and after three or four dates she'd commenced to push the marriage idea. Actually, she was in a frenzy to get married. A wild petter—she'd throw fits, completely black out. Come right down to it with Myra, she'd thrash and wail, sobbingly remind you what an upstanding man her dad was." He laughed bitterly. "Temple Drake loved to eat and have her cake! The sex act was a practical impossibility anyhow. Myra, knowing herself, her susceptibility, wore chastity gear when out on dates. Two or three sets of bloomers, and under that, something that felt like an iron corset."

Taylor's look was wry. "The marriage bans were forthwith posted, Papa Bentley proudly announced the pending event in the *Hollywood Reporter*, other papers please copy. He had gold-embossed invitations printed up, and tried to rent the Rose Bowl for the wedding ceremony. Failing that, Grauman's Chinese Theater, with all the hoopla of a première."

"Fade out Alec Taylor," Susan said at once.

Taylor nodded. "Two weeks before the nuptials, I copped off without notice or an exit speech. I holed up in a Frisco hotel with a case of Scotch, using a bogus name. I read books, sketched out story ideas, and developed a marvelous amnesia about iron-pants Myra. That is, until *Papa* Bentley caught up with me."

Taylor held up two fingers. "Private detectives paid me a surprise visit one afternoon. The next twenty-four hours were pretty incredible. Before Papa Bentley arrived, both private eyes worked me over like twin Sam Spades. They used rubber truncheons, beat me on the head, over the heart, then down around the really sensitive places. I'd conk out, then come to for a repeat of the same. And not a word said—I had the eerie feeling that I was being murdered by two deaf mutes."

Susan's eyes reflected horror, and Taylor said, "I'm actually *understating* it; but enough, dissolve. Scene now with Papa Bentley added to the cast. He interrogated me closely and fanatically, like that Inquisitor what's-his-name in Dostoevski? My fling with his daughter—he wanted a kiss-by-kiss account of it. I was made to describe it for

Papa in the most intimate detail, like a lurid sex novel. Had I opened her brassière, or otherwise disrobed Myra? Had I exposed myself, and did daughter Myra fondle my member? It went on sickeningly like that, from night till day, with Papa drinking up my Scotch and swearing my murder if I didn't confess to having devirginized and systematically ravished his daughter."

Taylor said after a silence, "On rainy days, I still feel that beating—certain resident areas of pain in my bones." He looked sharply at Susan. "I've kept a long-range eye on Papa Bentley in these intervening years—very curious about how a psychopath of his stripe would come out!"

"He came to some dreadful end," Susan said. "They locked him away."

Taylor shook his head. "He's Mr. Big today. Famous for his philanthropies, a power in the Church, an adviser to Presidents. Draw a moral from that!"

"I've never heard anything so frightful," Susan said in a sick tone. She put a hand up, as if wanting to call a halt to Taylor's account.

Taylor continued, oblivious to her reaction. "I looked up Helga mainly as a reaction to Myra. I'd had all I wanted of maidens of middle-class virtue—Helga, in contrast, was both a shining angel and an earth-woman. Finding Helga presented a problem. She'd moved as usual to dodge rent arrears, her pimp had lost track of her. I wrote her general delivery, White Fish, Montana, hoping the letter would somehow be forwarded to her. The letter was, and eventually Helga phoned me at the studio, as my letter requested. She was reluctant to make a date to see me; I had to pry her address from her. She was living in a furnished room in a slum area of Los Angeles."

A hoarseness crept into Taylor's tone now. "When we got together I found her pregnant. In her fifth month, and really bellied-out. She was on the welfare rolls, was getting prenatal help with the understanding that on delivery of the child she'd leave it with the Foundling Hospital for adoption." He cleared his throat noisily. "A city sanitation worker was footing the bills, standing by with his wife to adopt Helga's offspring legally. As a final thank-you, he was to give Helga two hundred dollars. Money to enable a fresh start and rehabilitation."

There was a long, sick silence, and then Taylor said, "I booted the childless couple out of the picture. When the child was born I named him Michael John, after my father."

Susan calculated in her mind. "Michael, then, is now fourteen."

"Come January." Taylor stared somberly at her. "Next episode tomorrow?"

She shook her head. "I'll hear the rest of it."

"All right, I married Helga. Almost at once. Took charge of her situation, took on responsibility for it. Ask me why, I'll give you a senseless answer."

"You believed the child she was bearing could be yours."

"I did not."

"You *knew* it could not be yours?"

"I was positive it wasn't."

"Then, in your own way, you were in love with Helga."

Taylor shook his head, denying it. "I was not. Nor was I really so moved at her plight. Her plight meant nothing to me—in fact, it would have been over for her in four short months."

Susan smiled faintly. "I'll hear your senseless answer now."

"Images of that week end in Tijuana were impressed on my mind. Like Helga's absolute joy over the dress and ratty fur stole I'd bought her. Also her simplicity as a woman—the way she could bend and twist into any form you liked. How you could animate her or erase her, according to your mood, your need of the hour.

"I married Helga to prevent my ever being trapped by a man-devouring bitch like Myra. I was a writer, with a few million words to get out—*the* main challenge ahead. A woman with a positive personality, your dynamic modern, would only drain off those creative energies, get me off the main track, involve me hopelessly in wasting side battles."

Susan said, "The answer isn't so senseless."

"No, I guess it isn't," Taylor said.

"Woman in her place," Susan said coldly. "Subject to the male whim, *so* grateful for small attentions. You weren't being so original in your choice of bride!"

Taylor squinted his eyes. "You sound angry."

"Your explanation of it was so prosaic, I'm amazed. I'd expected something quite brilliant and mystifying. You're a writer, after all."

Taylor grinned weakly. "See what I meant by being ambiguously the butcher and barber?"

Susan said slowly, "I had the peculiar feeling for a moment that I was hearing Richard. That it was not you, but Richard talking."

"Who is Richard?"

"Richard Harding!"

"Oh." He frowned. "Give me the kicker, go ahead."

163

"It's how Richard fancies women—how he wanted *me* to be. Complaisant, an amoeba." She turned her gaze fully on Taylor. "The main track"—she mimicked Taylor's voice—"and *the* really important life challenge. Richard used all your words."

"Blame assembly-line culture." Taylor stamped down his own anger. "You get your ideas at Rexall's, the counter between cosmetics and sporting goods. The next voice you hear is doing a mimicry of the last voice you heard." He smiled now. "You struggle all your life to preserve any one difference you have over the next fellow."

Susan laughed, helpless not to. "You've got your one difference," she said. "Words, what you can do with words."

"You say it like a certain nose-picking producer I used to hack for," Taylor said wryly. "Words. He'd phone and ask me, quote, to run him off some words, unquote. As if I were a tailor with fabric." He looked frowningly at her. "First thing on the agenda upstairs is the boot for your ex. I've been getting what-for because of him!"

She shook her head. "But I wasn't transferring hostility. Alec, you're being absurd."

"You did confuse the two of us before—lump us together."

"Not maliciously. But let's not go over and over it. I'd rather you finished your story."

"So cue me."

"You were married and an expectant father."

"Everything went fine for a few years, an even keel. The boy developed certain resemblances to me—pigmentation, general body structure, a hook to his nose, same blue-gray eyes. Surprisingly enough like me to make me wonder whether it *had* been my sperm. Helga kept house, was economical with money, adapted to my irregular eating habits, my foul temper when in the throes of a script.

"Trouble began when I caught on as a writer, began to make money. You think that's a paradox, you've never lived in Hollywood! I became really a pro; a few of my screenplays became top money grossers." Taylor smiled sourly. "Those are the magic words in Hollywood, the open sesame to the producer's heart *and* to the studio safe. *Top money grosser*—pap stories, not an original idea in them, conceived mainly to showcase glittering stars like Barbara Stanwyck, Melvyn Douglas, Irene Dunne. I got a salary hike to three thousand a week, and then when I became a free-lance or independent contractor, my price was a minimum twenty-five and up to forty thousand a script."

Taylor lit a cigarette and coughed with the first intake of smoke. "I said trouble began with prosperity—but I wasn't so aware of it then. Everything, in fact, seemed to brighten at first. The awful money pinch was over, certain necessaries and luxuries were obtainable. I bought a house, a late-model car, hired a housekeeper. I began to ease up, work more sensible hours, knock off week ends. And Helga began to blossom, but slowly, not *too* noticeably." He laughed harshly. "I don't really mean the word blossom, I mean *change*. She began to buy more clothes, more *expensive* clothes, visit beauticians, drive her own car, to dare to go out socially. Then she began to change more radically. She sponged up ideas, began to spout opinions on things, began to vie and compete with other women, flirt with men.

As she emerged, the Helga I'd married submerged, disappeared without a trace. Helga became Mrs. Alec Taylor, wife of a film-colony celebrity, but to the hilt!"

Taylor pursed his lips, then said with heavy irony, "Eight years after I'd fled to that hotel in Frisco, I found myself married to Myra Bentley!"

Susan asked, "Where is Helga today?"

He flared his cigarette, puffing furiously, and backed some steps into the gloom of the basement.

"Alec, where is she today?" Her tone was nervous now.

"She's dead."

Susan's blood was pounding now so she could hear it. She could think of nothing to say.

Taylor spoke rapidly from where he was in the shadows —"When the political cross fire began to hot up with Korea, Helga began to go to pieces. With the witch hunt, I became unemployed and unemployable. Also *persona non grata*, except for a few friends in a similar fix. My coventry became Helga's too. Her friends dropped away, she even got the brush from the service tradesmen. The milk and bread men stopped making deliveries. The maid quit, after painting the word Communists on the living-room wallpaper, and outside on the garage stucco. In a supermarket one day, a hysterical butcher accused Helga of having murdered his soldier son. In school, Michael was beaten up so regularly we had to withdraw him, get him private tutoring."

There was a long silence, then Taylor said, "It got even worse as turncoat after turncoat began to name me publicly. It was a rare week when my name didn't pop up in some congressional hearing." He smiled bitterly. "I became part of the accepted confession formula. Turncoats would name so many deceased writers, and Alec Taylor!"

Susan said, "Helga wanted you to give testimony and perhaps reinstate yourself. As others were doing."

"I said you'd hear it with a woman's ears!"

She frowned as if she didn't quite understand the thrust. Taylor said, "There was another assumption you could have made!" He shrugged. "Yes, I had to stand up to Helga *too*. We had some pretty rough scenes."

"What an awful nightmare for her," Susan said. "God, who wouldn't go to pieces!"

Taylor said intensely, "I lived in the same hell!"

"But with convictions." Susan fumbled in her mind. "You at least had that to sustain you."

Taylor kept to a hard silence, and soon Susan asked fearfully, "Did Helga kill herself?" She put a hand over her heart, in preparation against the reply she knew she would hear.

"She'd invited a couple to cocktails and dinner"—Taylor's voice was flat and unemotional—"a cabinetmaker who'd done work for us, and his wife. Helga needed the assurance of people calling on her, guests in the house. The couple arrived very late, after dark, and came in from the rear, avoiding the front door. They'd parked their car a half-mile away and then walked to our place. The F.B.I. was noting down the license numbers of cars parked on or near our driveway—anyhow, that was the fear of our guests. While they were having their drinks, Helga locked herself in the bathroom and swallowed poison."

There was an absolute silence, then Taylor said, "Michael is with my sister in East Chicago. He's bitter toward me, doesn't communicate with me. The therapist advises that for the time being, I do not write Michael or make any attempt to see him." He averted his eyes. "Once when I forced myself on the boy, he locked himself in a closet. When I broke the door down, I found him rigid, as if he'd had a stroke."

"Your son blames you for his mother's death?" There was a catch in her voice.

Taylor paced toward her. He demanded her eyes, then said, "And don't you?"

She was slow answering it. "No, I don't think I do."

Taylor looked surprised, and Susan said carefully, "People who commit suicide are inclined to it. Besides, she had a remedy of sorts. I mean, independently of you."

"Leave me," Taylor said at once. "Pick up and go."

Susan nodded. "Make another life for herself and Michael, away from you."

Taylor took her hand impulsively and pressed it gratefully. "There's a quality to you I like and admire." He was momentarily lost for a way to say it. "You try to be fair," he said finally.

He squeezed her hand, signaling a need for even greater reassurance, but she withdrew her hand from his grasp and he drew away stiffly. He tried unsuccessfully to mask his hurt, then said coldly, "*Now* make that speech you suppressed out of kindness!"

She looked at him uneasily. "I don't know what you mean."

"About what kind of man is it who will pull a whole world down for a dogma."

She shook her head. "It's in your mind, not mine."

"Come, your brain's agile enough to have thought of it."

She looked levelly at him. "It's your world and your

passions"—she gestured helplessly—"I can hardly understand it, or even *feel* it. It simply has no reality for me. I'm
essentially a provincial."

"Crap." Taylor smiled wisely. "You're as worldly as
anybody, Toots. Strike a Sweet Alice pose for me, I'll
laugh in your face."

She flushed but met his gaze steadily. "If you must beat
somebody—"

He said mockingly, "Save me from maidens up on their
pamphlet psychiatry!"

She went swiftly by him, to return upstairs as she'd
come, then reconsidered and stopped, waiting for Taylor
to join her on the stone stairs.

26

Lisa sat deep in the overstuffed chair, with Hertzig on the
arm of it where he could ogle her spilling breasts. Lisa said,
with drink-thickened speech, " *'Et tout ce que je ne sais
pas dire, tout ce que je ne connaitrai jamais, tout cela tout
cela changé en ce vin pur.'* " She smiled patronizingly at
Hertzig, and then completed the quotation: " *'Dont Paris
avait soif, me fut alors presenté.'* "

Hertzig said immediately, "Guillaume Apollinaire." He laughed at Lisa's surprised look. "The pure wine for which Paris was thirsty once upon a decade. *I* knew the old Paris you remember, Lisa—as a young man, I wore a borrowed full-dress suit to the Boeuf sur le Toit. I dined at tables and drank at the bar and admired painters, poets, musicians and writers."

"I was a child then," Lisa said. "Too young to go to the Boeuf sur le Toit."

"Of course." Hertzig sought to ingratiate himself. "You were hardly more than an infant in 1923; it is not possible that you were more than five years old."

"You don't have to be gallant, or such a liar," Lisa said. "I'm forty-nine—anyhow, underage for the Boeuf sur le Toit in 1923." She reached wantonly into the bosom of her dress, whisked a hand about, then drew out a toilet tissue. She saw Hertzig's tantalized eyes. "You really should arrange with a woman, Victor—" She laughed.

Hertzig shifted his legs embarrassedly. "I have been married three times. Each marriage only proved that I am unable to support a wife."

Lisa's eyes swept his puny figure and she said teasingly, "Then become a eunuch, why be tormented?"

Hertzig first reddened, and then smiled foolishly. "It's famine and then feast, and then famine again. My luck in love is the same as any bachelor's."

Lisa frowned, searching back into her own thoughts. "It was open house always, with Eva presiding. I watched and listened avidly, and when I was ordered upstairs to bed, I listened through the walls, lay with an ear to the floor, hearing the tumult of laughter and the wonderful conversation. God, God oh God, how the voices and names come

170

back to me! Cocteau, Picasso, Marie Laurencin, Massine, the poet Louis Aragon, Maurice Rostand. Victor, damn you, look more impressed! And René Clair, and Erik Satie, the hermit musician of Arcueil."

Hertzig said, "They couldn't all be your mother's lovers."

"Victor, how amazed you would be if I named the ones!"

Hertzig stared quizzically, and Lisa said luminously, "I'd hear them with my mother in the bedroom adjoining mine. The gaiety and laughter, the sound of champagne glasses, and then the significant silence. I was twelve—it was theater to me, an incomparable theater!"

Hertzig said, "At twelve, I worked at the ovens making bread. My father had suffered a paralytic stroke, and I stood in his place. This was in Rumania."

Lisa said, "Laurencin drew three poses of my mother on the dining-room wall. In colored chalks, then sprayed with fixative." She struck her brow. "God, if the new occupants have painted over that wall!"

"Paint out a fortune in Art?" Hertzig shook his head.

"Victor, I've got to get my house back!" She said it in a child's voice of panic.

Hertzig said superfluously, knowing the answer as he did, "It was seized for taxes, and then sold at auction."

Lisa nodded miserably.

"You have the memories," Hertzig consoled. "*They* were not sold in the auction."

"The memories, yes." Lisa brightened and went on with her reminiscences. "The love poems to Eva! Victor, I have them in my trunk even today! And Isadora Duncan!" she cried exultantly. "She'd visit us, and stay for weeks and weeks. I called her aunt, on her insistence. She'd bring me

171

such wonderful presents—miniature *teatro dell'arte* figures on a toy revolving stage once, and another time a huge Easter egg with figurines of the Russian royal family inside the egg."

"And Isadora's admirers?" Hertzig winked. "Did she visit with a full entourage?"

"Her admirers, of course." Lisa laughed gaily. "Love was an ingredient of her genius, she was fierce about love." Her eyes closed now and her face whitened as if she'd fainted.

Hertzig leaned over to whisper yearningly in her ear. "Is there a chance for me, will there ever be a time for me?"

She opened her eyes and looked frankly at him. "Yes," she said. "There will inevitably be a time for you." A laugh locked in her throat. "The way the world turns, I'll one day be eager for Victor Hertzig." Her fingers ran ticklingly along Hertzig's thigh. "A drink, Victor, please. Be a darling and get it for me."

27

There was the scent of jasmine in the air—Susan sniffed the fragrance testingly, like a buyer sampling at a perfume counter. She'd come to the ground-level patio with an urgent need for space, a squirrel escaping a cage. Her mind was tumultuous with Taylor, the sick, oppressive truth of him. She'd come to the patio alone to regather herself, evict Taylor from her thoughts, free her mind of the clutter of him, so she could again concentrate on herself, her own dilemma in living.

The foliage banking the ground-level patio etched scalloped patterns on the walls of the villa. Off where the public road crossed the private one in a T, the passing scene looked to Susan curiously like panoramic sequences on a narrow screen. Natives marched across the screen in an epic of time: first an elder, slow as if toiling uphill, the straw sombrero worn so the profile began with the nose; then his wife, hardly behind, one arm out rodlike and a parrot perched on it. The progeny followed in broken line, down to the grandchildren, with an old dog between them sneezing up the dust, and last a burro on hobbled legs.

She was busy with the theme of herself again, when she saw Harding stroll toward her. Her first wild impulse was to run, dart into some newer sanctuary, before he could trap her. And then Harding was right beside her—enclosing her, as Taylor had a while ago, and looking at her demandingly, a cigarette held between clenched teeth, and lines in his cheeks that made his face smaller.

She eyed him first meanly. Then her face slowly opened into a smile, as if across the years. A smile warm and cold, an acknowledgment, if nothing more, of their long time together.

Harding puffed his cigarette silently, in a subtle transfer of the burden of talk to her. He stared up briefly at a procession of sunset clouds marching across the sky, and then looked back to her.

In a way she was glad now that Harding had elected to corner and confront her. He was more than anything an old friend, and she was wretchedly lonesome in this battle with herself. Also, she was becoming once more unsure, as rudderless as she'd been before this new freedom.

"You want more of a story," she began, slowly marshaling those resources of courage and boldness the next minutes would require. She laughed. "I'm quoting your own words."

Harding nodded calmly, and Susan said, "If it's been a secret, I've kept it reluctantly." Her eyes held his. "You could have gotten the story from me any time you liked. My story, just for the asking!"

Harding flushed. "I get around to things late."

"Where does one begin?" She was remote for some moments, then she turned her gaze fully on him. "Have you any idea *how* I celebrated my thirty-eighth birthday, Richard?"

He looked surprised at the question. "June, let me see? Yeah, June twentieth." He rummaged hurriedly in his mind. "Sure thing. We made it a foursome with the Applebys. Dinner in town, and then a show." He smiled now. "What did I give you, let me think? Sure—that string of pearls."

"That was the June before."

Harding said quickly, "The antique brooch with the garnets. *No,* that was for the anniversary." He smiled apologetically. "Senility. My memory's shot to hell."

Susan said, "The foursome with the Applebys happened a week *after* my birthday."

"Oh, did it?" He floundered, "Some good reason for that, no doubt. Trouble getting theater tickets, or, as usual, some damned crisis in the office—"

Susan said, "I sat in Balfour's on my birthday. At the outside café tables. I had lunch alone."

Harding stared blankly. "Balfour's up on Hawthorne Road?"

Susan nodded. "I wore a tight dress slit at the side that showed off my legs. And high heels, the highest I could find at Delson's. I had my hair in a feather cut—"

Harding said slowly, "I remember the feather cut. Damned cute, really damned cute."

Susan said, "You'll find a corridor of women every lunchtime at Balfour's. Widows, divorcées, and some wives. All over thirty-five, and some over fifty. All of them overpainted and in clothes too young for them."

A muscle jumped in Harding's cheek. "What're you getting at?"

"I sat among them. Hoping to be seen, and admired. Competing with them for male admiration. Hoping to be chosen, that some passing driver would smile, and stop his car." Her eyes on him were cold and flat. "That's how I really celebrated my thirty-eighth birthday."

Her face was empty. "You watch for the finer, more expensive cars. You'd prefer a man of your own station, with a veneer of breeding. A common language; some exchange of ideas along with the other thing. But after a while you look straight at the older, cheaper cars, the Fords, Plymouths and Chevrolets."

Harding laughed artificially, avoiding her eyes. "An afternoon pickup in suburbia—what lucky fellow is that unemployed?"

"Those men who know about Balfour's, who've shopped there successfully before, or who have been told about it, the way men pass the word along." She laughed harshly. "Why, Balfour's outside patio is famous. Or don't I mean notorious."

She waited for him ask the question she anticipated. She watched him struggle to repress it, and soon she said, "Other secret afternoon vices of the unloved suburban wife—" She looked levelly at him. "Want to hear it?"

"It's what you tell the priest or the analyst," Harding said uncomfortably. "But sure, go ahead with it. Get it said."

"This has its ritual." She sighed. "A negligee in a darkened bedroom. The blinds drawn and the draperies closed to shut out the sun, give the illusion of night. Your lover is a television personality, a smiling master of ceremonies. Or the handsome leading man in an old movie." Her voice shook a little. "If you're lucky, it's Humphrey Bogart, or David Niven."

Harding's eyes were shocked. Susan said, "I once wore my black lace evening dress, the Schiaparelli we bought in Paris."

"The time of our honeymoon." Harding nodded mechanically.

"When I took it off, I burned it in the fireplace." She waited for his eyes. "I'd first torn it to shreds."

There was a silence, and then Susan said, "You never asked about my Wednesdays, or were the least bit curious—"

"It was your day in town, that break in the week." Harding gestured. "You drove in to shop, do the art galleries—" She was shaking her head, and he stopped.

Susan said, "I had a weekly appointment. At the found-ling ward of the New York Hospital."

Harding's eyes were round with astonishment. Susan said, "I'd applied and was accepted. Wednesday from eleven to eleven forty-five was my time to fondle a found-ling."

Harding looked as if he didn't understand. Susan said, "The babies needed human warmth, to be fussed over and loved, more than the few nurses could possibly provide." Her voice dropped. "There were more applicants than the supply of babies. Women and wives without a baby of their own. I waited six months to be called."

Harding reached impulsively to take her hand. Susan avoided his touch. She spoke away from him, her stare fixed on the panorama of people and livestock up where the public road made its T. "Childless women separate from their friends, those that have children. The friendship be-comes increasingly artificial and pointless. The mother is full of the joy of it, and you're sick with jealousy."

Harding said, "God in heaven, there are more childless couples!"

"But never right next door." Susan smiled bleakly. "I had the Bronsons with two children, and the Dunphys with three, both right next door. And the Gilers directly across the road with how many tricycles on the lawn?" She shook her head. "Childless women have to seek each other out, in-conveniently and across distances."

"But that's only in the suburbs," Harding objected.

"But I lived in the suburbs!" She closed her eyes, then opened them very wide. "I lived with the sounds of other people's children. Overheard their games and quarrels, lay awake nights with their cries and illnesses."

Harding mopped his brow and cheeks, then blew noisily into the handkerchief. "My season for sniffling," he said.

She responded automatically, by rote. "You have your allergy pills?"

He nodded. "In my briefcase. Enough for a couple of days."

Susan laughed suddenly. The exchange was an index of their basic married dialogue for how many years. Pills, his and hers; a togetherness of hay fever, heartburn, cramps, constipation. A partnership in capsules, Bromo-Seltzer, suppositories.

She said, "I spent some of my time constructively." She smiled at Harding's uneasy stare. "Did you know that I took courses in basket weaving, in ceramic sculpture, in jewelry making? That I joined a Yoga group one year, and when Zen Buddhism became popular, I gave my time to that?"

Harding said, "You were sold on Dianetics the last I knew."

"*Ten* years ago."

He said heavily, "God, but does tempus fugit!" He grasped at another item in the backwash. "Then there was that Wilhelm Reich bit. Did I get his name right? The Conovers converted you to that." He laughed involuntarily. "You sat in a box and cured a wart, was it?"

Susan said, "You provided too royally. The house ran itself, and I could only be in the way." She looked gravely at him. "You do pathetic things to fill the time. But you wouldn't know."

Harding shook his head slowly. "Never enough time for me. Days whiz by too damned fast." He caught himself, and added contritely, "But that's the business world for you. A crazy battleground where time is priceless ammunition."

She accepted a cigarette from Harding's pack, then inclined her chin to the gold-dipped mechanical lighter. Her eyes remarked on the lighter—it had been her gift to him, sent to him overseas sometime during those twenty-two months she'd been an army wife.

Harding saw her look. He bounced the lighter on his palm. "I had Dunhill repair it the other week. It's as good as new." He coughed the huskiness out of his tone. "You've dished up a lot of stuff. I don't know what to chew on first." He added, "It's on me, to a great extent my fault. You've been implying it, and, well, okay, I'm chiefly the villain."

Susan said quickly, "There are no villains."

Harding stared in surprise. "*That* . . . is a hunk of wisdom!"

Susan smiled slightly. "It's the first time you've ever thought me wise, about anything." She dropped the cigarette for him to step on. "You were you, as good as you are, and as bad as you are. It was the best possible world for you, the worst possible one for me. I had a bad marriage; I was married to the wrong man. And for so long, it was almost too late for anything."

Harding said emotionally, "I had no idea you were that miserable."

"I felt old and unattractive, and so demoralized. And tormented daily, by movies, newspaper stories, television commercials—wherever youth was adored and adulated." She laughed hollowly. "I was depressed by Kim Novak, slaughtered by Sophia Loren." Her laugh caught in a sob. "I'd catch you looking at my face critically, as if comparing it with some other. I didn't dare cold cream my face nights, put my hair up in curlers, do the normal things. I grew ashamed of my body, ashamed to stand naked before you."

Harding said something unintelligibly in his throat. Susan's voice thinned. "Varicose bursts on my thighs. I'd die before I'd let you see them."

Harding found his voice to say protestingly, "You're really laying it on! I never in any way slighted your womanhood—you simply projected your own fears."

Susan said, "I *knew* the comparisons you were making this last year."

"How's that again?" He stared intensely at her, then said, "Oh, I see." There was an edge in his tone now. "There was only *one* way you could know, ever find out!"

She nodded her head. "Call me cheap," she said indifferently. She met his look calmly. "The detective drooled describing her. As other detectives had other times."

Harding said, "You really went for broke with detective agencies?"

"I had to do it." Her face shadowed. "So I'd know my husband, not live with a complete stranger."

She turned her back to him, moved forward on the patio, looking out to the T of the road. The sky was darkening faster now, with rainbow effects like flame falling to the earth. A woman in an embroidered skirt carrying a floral wreath and a basket of fiesta delicacies crossed the screen, and soon after her, a man with a wooden crucifix like a workman's tool balanced over his shoulder. The screen was blank, and then two little girls, plump and merry, with wide crepe-paper bows in their hair, scampered across.

Harding spoke from behind her. "Must be a cemetery somewhere up the road. Damned if I can understand how people can make a carnival out of death."

Susan shifted her glance to a gnarled, century-old olive tree impaled against the half-light. She said, "As I grew older, you picked younger and younger mistresses."

She heard Harding speak behind her. "I did what other men do. I'm no worse than anybody."

She turned back to him. When their eyes met, she said, "I went to see the last one. Not in anger, but to determine what she could give you beside her youth. I found her sympathetic, not hard or coarse, as I'd expected." She nodded to Harding's look of absolute surprise. "She gave me her opinion of you, the sort of man she'd found you to be. And advice on how to handle you, hold you. She was getting married, she told me, and wondering how to break the news to you. When I told her I didn't think I wanted to hold you, she looked sad."

Harding was silent. Susan said, "I felt even more despondent after the visit. I now knew the woman you could endure and even make love to. I wasn't like her, not at all, nor ever could be."

They crossed the patio, as if to return to the salon. Harding said, "We sure saved up a lot of dirty laundry."

She stopped and said, "There's more, Dick. Bales of it. Yours *and* mine."

He looked at her closely. "Burn the lot of it," he said buoyantly. "Just like you burned that lace gown."

She shook her head. "It won't work. I mean, it won't work for us."

"Hell, you can lose the rest of your life in the laundry!"

She said intensely, "You really lose it by lying and glossing over." *By hiding the dirt* phrased itself burningly in her mind.

Her eyes turned fully on him. "You're not really so blithe as you pretend!"

"What's behind that dig?"

"Interpret it as you like."

"Is there a bigger dossier somewhere?"

When Susan didn't answer, Harding said gruffly, "I underrated you. What happened to the cute dumb bunny?"

Susan laughed despite herself. "She grew old, and peculiar."

"And *over*analytical!"

She picked up the gauntlet. "The *hard* way. I had to do it for myself."

He stared glumly at her. "All I got for my time on the couch was a pain. Brant egged me into it; I went mainly because of old man Brant. To humor the dictatorial sonofabitch, keep peace in the firm."

He saw her skeptical look and said defensively, "It was that year of my damned insomnia, you remember. I was at low ebb, physically and mentally, fed up with life and stuff. And drinking; bottles stashed everywhere. Brant played Dutch uncle, and when that didn't take, he shoved me over on Barshak. Barshak'd once helped a fellow Brant knew over a crisis, and Brant consequently had a lot of faith in him. But Barshak was a waste of time. He tried everything he could to make me dependent on him." He smiled grimly. "I was a meal ticket. And a wedge into Madison Avenue trade; Barshak could name-drop me when recruiting other balmy executives."

Her brows were still raised, and Harding said irritably, "That crack before about 'doing it for yourself.' Hell, I never counted out money to you—what stopped you from seeing an analyst?"

Susan said quietly, "I'd begun interviewing doctors— and then I came here instead." She looked steadily at him. "Like you, I was appalled by the bales of dirty laundry. I ran off and left them behind, just as you did when you quit Barshak."

He angled his head to hide his eyes and lit a cigarette. He said stiffly, "Your articulate friend in there. Is it an affair, or for real?"

She didn't answer.

"You'll have worse trouble than you knew," Harding said. "Don't be too charmed by his brilliance. He's a pathological case—you won't make out with him. You'll be hurt."

Susan looked at him in sharp surprise. Harding said, "He made a bet on history and lost. Now he wants to pull the world down with him." He saw her surprise now and smiled. "I'm not a boob in every department." He shrugged. "Maybe that Mex divorce *is* as permanent as any . . . But even so, I'm for you, I'm a friend." He walked briskly ahead of her, back to the salon.

28

Hertzig held Lisa's hand in a lock of fingers, to hold her in place. They were sitting flank to flank, sharing the wide, stuffed chair. He watched her warily, keeping his jaw angled away from her bobbing head. He'd been injured twice already, with a small tasting of blood. He wanted to steal away, to privately examine his bridge and rinse his mouth, but opportunity held him. They were finally breaking common ground, he felt; the building plot for that mausoleum they would share in some tomorrow, very soon. Old acquaintances in platonic union, both of them clasped at twilight's end, swapping reminiscences and remembered laughter. He wanted it like that—Lisa in exactly that measure and no more of her. Lisa with her fires banked, done with today and tomorrow, vital only in her recollections, full up with yesterday.

He looked sidewise at her. When would the phenomenal charge fizzle out, the batteries go dead? Or did a woman's sex drive accelerate in that season when a man's began to wane and tire? He'd found this biological paradox true more often than he cared to remember, than ego permitted him to remember.

Lisa's head bobbed fitfully, like a cork riding turgid seas, and Hertzig jumped up to prevent the blow. She said disconnectedly, back again in her reveries, "Nothing to do but amuse yourself and love the arts. And that Balot, never serious, what wonderful buffoonery! He'd talk, and I'd write it down—I kept a notebook. A favorite of a great designer . . . my mother stole him away. Through Balot, Eva met Stravinsky, and Prince Georges Ghika. And Captain Molyneux, and Marcel Raval, founder of *Feuilles libres*.

"And Raoul, the art critic, so elegant and influential!" The voice was almost lost. "He was my first lover. He'd quarreled with Eva. When she closed her door to him, he stole into my room. I was fifteen. At breakfast, Eva laughed over it, not a bit jealous of me. But she never took him back, or invited him back, and I never saw him again."

Her head nodded, then slumped down to her chest. Hertzig leaned over and kissed the nape of her neck.

BOOK TWO

1

In the first seconds of the earthquake, there were small vibrations in the Villa de la Soledad. Of minor notice, mainly ignored by the eating guests, as if these were but the waves of some faraway explosion or car collision. A taboret lurched, windows rattled, a plate fell from a kitchen shelf, in a glass exhibit case a bell with enameled ornamentation rang mysteriously.

In the early seconds, there was a cascading of coal on the roof, as if a chimney had fallen.

The hi-fi stopped its music as the diamond needle suddenly skipped its groove. The recording left unfinished was Duke Ellington's "A Train."

Janoff, with his plate of *boeuf bourguignon* balanced on his lap, and eating hungrily, jolted so the fork stabbed his tongue.

Below, in the airless cellar quarters where the servants lived, the tints of light on the concrete walls erased when all the tapers unexplainably blew out. The peasants who saw this, the three women, stopped their hymns. They stood mute and huddled together, struck dumb by the phenomenon. Soon the infant at their feet began to slap the floor and wail his frustration—he couldn't see where he'd dropped his death's head of sugar.

The first real alarm in the salon commenced when one of the huge crystal chandeliers fell in a rain of jewels. As if by signal, the guests screamed in unison.

On the highest terrace, Max Marsant watched the dry hard ground of the highland slope become molten and move sinuously like quicksand. Then it engulfed him in giant, swelling waves, filling his mouth, ears, nose, as the full force of the earthquake struck the Villa de la Soledad. There was no time for a last thought, or an outcry. Max was at once mercifully dead, as if, simultaneous with the earth convulsion, his heart had stopped.

The villa shook to its foundation; giant cracks formed in the outside walls as if running from the body of the earth. The walls caved in with a beast-roar, quickly and on all sides. The avalanche of earth and masonry bounding from the steep-sided promontories overran the villa, forming a sea around it that closed the entrances and exits and sealed in the ruins.

Inside the villa itself, there were sequences of flashing red, blue and purple flame in the rooms as light bulbs blew and fixtures short-circuited. When total darkness settled, there was the pervasive and nose-stinging odor of burning wires. Ceilings and the interior walls dropped in chunks like a rockslide; beams fell vertically, as if toppled by a woodsman's ax. As water pipes broke, there were sounds of rushing waters, numerous streams charging through the villa. Moaning cries came from the trapped, maimed and injured; and prayers, unintelligibly rendered with the words running together. A medley of sounds that fell deafly on the ears of the dead.

Harry Archer was dead. Face down on the floor in a

forward crouch, as if felled in flight by a rock propelled from a giant sling. He lay neat in his clothes, with that dandified look that was his style. Only the back of his head was unsightly.

Victor Hertzig was dead. He lay with his eyes open and thrusting from the sockets and his face contorted in shock. What had actually killed Hertzig needed later determination. Small as he'd been, he looked even smaller in death. Puppet-small and toylike beside the upended furniture that fenced him off from the others in the salon.

Leona was dead. Entombed in the kitchen with the two native cooks, sealed in awfully with the debris.

2

In the low-lying Choluca hub, the death toll and devastation were frightful. Separate fires, fanned into one huge conflagration by a northeast wind, made a wall of fire that divided the village in half. Those buildings that still stood were mainly unroofed, or stripped of their façades, or aslant and half in the earth. A dense pall of smoke hung in the atmosphere like a gray shroud. People crawled rodentlike through the blackened skeletons of dwellings and in the wreckage looking for lost relatives, foraging for bits and scraps of their belongings. Some of them, forgetting speech, imitated the cries of wounded animals.

A man in the upper story of a building split exactly in two leaped so he lay impaled on the prongs of a standing picket fence.

A man clawed out of a deep crevice in the earth, to stand naked and bleeding and eyeless. He found fellows by sound and touch, grasping at their clothes, to babble the miraculous happening of his survival.

The mass of survivors ran around bereft, clutching crucifixes and images of saints, lost to any logical understanding of the horror, since all reason and sanity was premised on the stability of the ground underfoot, that it remain firm and true and motionless.

Some of the more maddened ran at each other with bared teeth and fists, in mutual attribution of blame for the holocaust.

There were some at the streams, men and women with scorched faces and bodies seeking space in the clogged waters. A grandmother stolidly held a badly burned child by the feet, head down in the water. Then, soon, a holy relic was thrown after the drowned child, in a rebuke to the Maker.

Groups in panicked flight on the roads found an impasse of ruins and smashed vehicles. Some known roads had disappeared; the contour of certain ground was incredibly different. On the high north boundary, a continuous line of precipitate rocks nearly a mile in length had tumbled down, to lie as vaulting barriers on roads that had connected with the great Pan-American Highway.

The Galería Tajín was not to be found. The massive

wreckage now strewn on its spot had once been the Hospital Santa Rosa, a four-story pink stucco edifice.

In the high hills of the Choluca cemetery, where the graves had been decorated for that night's feast and fun, the earth's violent exgurgitation had thrown up coffins. Human skeletons lay exposed in the soft furrows of earth. Those early-comers who had survived the earth-shock screamed terribly in their first revulsion for the dead. Some threw earth at the skeletons, or stamped them back into the ground with their feet. A few others dropped dead as the sights they saw became unbearable. In a remarkable chemical reaction to the unearthed dead, the hair of a twenty-year-old youth turned snow-white at once, as if a patent bleach had been poured on it.

The Church San Felipe was unroofed now; its altars and saints were rubble. Only the massive walls stood. Father Porfirio was a casualty: blood ran from an ear, his body was badly bruised and both his legs were broken. He had lain under debris, slowly suffocating; and then, adventitiously, the gnome-sized caretaker Joachim appeared to rescue him. Joachim himself was unhurt; by a quirk of circumstance, he had been flung through a window to fall thirty feet to the patio below without a broken bone or any visible damage—a miracle, this, that the pious Joachim was later to relate over and over, as case in proof of that more benevolent and judicious side of the Lord.

When his faculties were reordered, and he understood the full calamity, Father Porfirio commanded Joachim to wheel him in a cart. Before leaving San Felipe, Father Porfirio said prayers for the dead in the church. Then outside, with Joachim wheeling him and holding a crucifix

high, the priest roamed the choked streets and alleys tirelessly, exhorting the sufferers, giving comfort to countless, and confessing and absolving the dying. In the ex-
altation of his task, Father Porfirio forgot the agony in his
body and legs. In some reserve of his mind, however, the
priest wondered how best to interpret and then convey the
meaning of the earthquake. When the sheer science of it
insinuated itself into his thinking, he resolutely shut his
mind to it. When some wretches screamed at him, questioning the Lord's wisdom, Joachim scolded them and beat
them off with a stick.

3

It was as if giant thumbs were gouging out his eyes. Taylor
had had this same sensation once before—in Tarragona,
Spain, in 1938, in the pitch-dark of a wartime shelter. He'd
been a demobilized infantryman then, but somehow unable
to quit Spain and go home; he'd stayed on, ragged and
joined tragically with the native civilians, moving with
the refugee hordes, fascinated by the day-to-day drama.

With the humans in the shelter were crates of fowls and
rabbits. When the Rebel bombs fell, the uprights, rafters

and roof of the shelter splintered and collapsed. A mother crouched beside him held her baby's mouth open, so that the concussions on the infant's ears would not burst his eardrums or collapse his lungs.

He'd lain trapped and sightless in that other wreckage, but optimistic about survival. He was young then, and this was his buoyancy.

He was not so convinced of survival now. In a depth of himself, he had for some time sensed Choluca to be his graveyard. He'd come to Choluca a dying man, psychologically rather than physiologically, in the way some men mysteriously die. And intensely wanting that death, the marvelous oblivion.

Where he lay in the salon, he could feel the debris rimming his body; a rummage pile of rough stone and broken glass oddly smooth as if every edge had been beveled and polished. He could hear his heart thumping like a hammer with a nose of hard rubber. His rib cage hurt excruciatingly, as if the bones inside were standing up and lancing through the flesh. From just below his hips and down to his toes there was hardly any sensation, as if death had crept so far. He tried to guess the substance of his injuries and his true condition, but in a while he gave up. He lay impatient for apathy and mindlessness—wonderful if he could go to sleep!

But it came over him again. Sharp in his senses as twenty years before; keen now as then, in the assault on the logic of his mind.

He was not Alec Taylor, but *Will Brooks*, in this reminiscence. For the fun of it, he'd signed up as a recruit using the name of a former teacher. To seed tomorrow with humor; so he could imagine the staid old pedagogue face in the muck, lighting signal flares on the battlefield, and so perhaps lighten those times of anxiety, uncertainty and fear. There had been a howling harvest of laughter—he'd many times stood the porcine Mr. Brooks in the battle line of the Fifteenth Brigade, Lincoln-Washington Battalion. He'd watched Brooks soldier for Taylor in the Ebro bridgehead, cackled over the cartoon of Brooks with his scaly lips and the ever ready camphor-ice stick, and the scalloped hair like a mane over the nape of his neck.

It had been fine fun, an inspired alias; good for deep belly laughs, and an old score to an extent repaid. But at the end of it, after the four months, as the offensive that would redeem Teruel became no more than a grim delaying action against the Fascists, he became Will Brooks, not by alias but truly. By new birth, blood, sacrifice, conspiracy, and by political murder.

They'd fought brilliantly but hopelessly against odds of forty men to one, ten guns to one, five planes to one; against air armadas that were black clouds of death, and against the tanks, the nine Spanish and Moorish divisions, the three Italian divisions.

Against six counteroffensives, finally to retreat before the seventh.

He reviewed that *murder* now, frank in his mind about it, and accepting it by name for what it had been. For what he now knew it to have been. He reconjured it in two scenes: the conspiratorial arrangement for it, and then the act of killing.

The enemy artillery and air barrage had filled the seven hours of unslept night. Huddling in the shelter, he'd listened dumbly, with horror, to Lieutenant Colonel Igor

Rotha, an International commander. Rotha had up to then posed as a noncombatant adviser in mufti, using the ridiculous alias of Gómez. Now, in the crisis before retreat, Rotha had openly taken a uniform, military rank, and a Russian name possibly his own. When Taylor had at last understood Rotha's guarded instructions, he'd assented with his eyes, helpless to refuse. Then he'd watched Rotha stop elsewhere in the shelter, going from man to man, covertly instructing on the up-coming morning slaughter of defeatists and political dissenters.

Just after dawn, while Savoia-Marchettis like gleaming white eagles strafed the bridgehead before the final break-through of enemy tanks and motorized artillery, Taylor had nervelessly trained his rifle sight on the back of a man in the forward line, and unerringly made the kill. The deed accomplished, he'd looked around for those others he'd watched Rotha instruct. He'd been able to witness three other brutal executions.

As a hundred times before, Taylor groped in his mind for the name of his victim. He'd blocked it out; but he was clear on certain incidental biography and personality. The man he'd murdered had been a Chicagoan, hardly twenty-five, skeletally thin and asthmatic, a former encyclopedia salesman, an unpublished poet, a man in the Chicago chapter of the John Reed Club, the son of an immigrant father who'd been a Wobbly and a disciple of Mikhail Bakunin, the nineteenth-century anarchist. They'd talked in what lulls they could find—the cautious, masking phrases of two strangers feeling each other out, both loath to show the other a too-defined and immutable intellectual self. The captain had been a hungry reader of books; he'd slogged from Teruel to the Ebro with a knapsack crammed with books and pamphlets. He'd lent Taylor one of his treasured books, Malcolm Cowley's *Exile's Return*. The book had never been returned—he'd still been reading it, excited by it and burning to discuss it, that morning he'd trained his rifle on the lender's back.

He'd seen Lieutenant Colonel Rotha, alias Gómez, one last time after the Ebro debacle. When for Loyalist policy reasons, the Brigade had been inactivated and finally demobilized, he'd wandered the ravished land as a non-combatant, tangentially away from the coastline, and finally to Catalonia. A rootless and unassigned observer and reporter, taking notes, forming impressions—he'd write a book, he thought; and in that perhaps clarify his own confusions, forge some belief and faith he could hold to. *Lay the ghost of the murdered captain*—perceive that "historical necessity" Rotha had pressed on him as the *raison d'état* of his deed.

The last encounter with Rotha happened in a wine-cellar headquarters in Catalonia. He'd taken emergency refuge during a severe aerial bombardment, to find himself in a huge cellar dug into a hill. There were peasants and soldiers jam-packed in the cellar, hilarious with wine, drugged against the terror riding the skies.

In the haven, he had not immediately recognized Rotha. The Russian was out of uniform again, with certain small alterations in his appearance. The mustache was shaved off, the hair cropped to bristles and dyed a tomato-red. With the façade of austerity and aloofness fallen, Rotha was acting gregariously, a fellow among fellows. He was guzzling straight from a bottle, his cheeks flaming and the sweat on him suet-thick and steaming. And he was laughing out loud, in oddly regulated bursts, as if telling himself one whopping joke over and over in the stops.

When he'd made Rotha aware of him, the Russian broke the neck of a champagne bottle against a wall, then thrust it at a Spanish infantryman to pass along to him. He'd drunk, with his eyes passionately on Rotha in a recklessly. open show of the distrust he felt for the Russian. Rotha'd met his look in kind, his face distorted with contempt, and then the chortling laugh, as if he, Taylor, fit that joke the Russian had been telling himself.

Taylor tried now to still his mind, draw tight covers over the storage in it, dam up the threatening seepage. Wait out that death that was being held over him as a boon, that reward for confession and self-damning, the repudiation of the whole of his life.

He'd been through the jazz before, he reminded himself with hard resolve. It was a pattern he was inured to: the star chamber, and an interrogator. This one invisible, a flogging voice in his head, but the same questions, the unchanging demands: confess, recant, mewl, slaver, decry the covenant of your faith; heap dung on your life commitment, the gospel and storm of your youth, the hard substance of your maturity. Call your truth a falsehood, call it supreme rationalization, call your life a lie, the whole pig-blind, sinful, pitiful time of it.

Taylor moved slightly, his neck and head only, for the feel of objects on his cheek. He tried to distinguish the masonry from the glass; to repossess some of himself by the hard device of touch, diminish the awesome limbo.

This was the final trap for mortals. The uneasy dark and

199

the bed of fear, the flesh inert and the victim stifling in the coventry of his mind. It was what kept priests in business, and God—the confession coffin and the Presence.

He squeezed his eyes tightly, wanting to dream into death.

No lamentations, not a one; no apologies, not a damned apology. He'd lived right as any man, and with more consistency. *One* course undeviatingly, from his youth to now, right through the calendar of his time. A man was to be honored for the absolute in him; damn it to hell, it was the stuff of greatness.

4

They were blue, twinkling stars, then eyes. When the creature stood identifiably on his chest, Vito screamed terribly in his throat. When he felt the sharp teeth pierce like prongs of a fork, he tried desperately to rise. There was an unbearable pain in his back; it felt broken. He lay very still now, his elbows in his sides, not to worsen his back injury. Soon he brought his assaulted wrist to his mouth; gnawed and sucked deeper than the bite until he tasted blood. When he guessed he had purified the wound as much as he could, he stopped. Now, in a belated reaction, he went green and sick. He shifted his head and lay open-mouthed and panting over the floor, drooling and unable to expel.

Soon now, Vito felt that he was suffocating. The chronic symptoms acutely back: unbearable pressures in his chest stopping breath. People walking on his chest, cars driving over him; he was lying prostrate under a crowd and was being trampled.

He felt along his side slowly to where his pocket was. When he found the crucifix, he brought it to his lips. *God in Heaven*—Vito prayed whimperingly behind the crucifix. A hobbled speech, and the prayers naïve and made-up.

In the conjuration of God, Vito's prayers at once stopped. He saw an angry face, for the benign one he wished.

The punishment is now—Vito interpreted the anger he saw. I'll rot here, crippled and helpless—be eaten by the rats.

He stared into the blackness, forcing vision so he could discern the bulking forms of rafters and beams, the debris heaping mountainously, the off-angled fixtures, furnishings and walls. He strained his ears to detect sounds, *any* sounds —the stir of bodies, moans, the sound of breathing.

They're all dead, he concluded finally. All of them, and Donna too.

Cowering before the angry face again, he had a haunted thought: *I was the bad luck, the curse*. They're all dead, and Vito Avedon is to blame.

It showed vividly now, flashing in that awesome face he watched. That horror that had made him sick beyond all healing, evil beyond any redemption. Fated for this punishment come now.

He heard the engine bells again—faint to his ears and dirgelike, muffled in yesterday. Then the breaking of glass, hardly sharper than crackling cellophane.

He saw himself in the grasp of a helmeted fire fighter. Small and bodiless, as if flesh and fat had burned off in the inferno. High on a rescue ladder, and the faces below slowly moving eye to eye with him as if the earth platform was rising on hydraulic hoists.

He stood on the street once more, croupily coughing blue smoke in the cold January air, looking down at the half-figure of Father Bonnard on his knees in the slush. He saw his people darkly, as through blind patches on his eyes. They lay in a row on the ground, outlined under heavy canvas covers. He counted in his head to *five*, as he'd done then and all the years since, going from the peculiar form of his crippled father to the littlest figure that had to be Tommy.

His uncle Guido had accused him in the deaths, and he had made no denial.

The kerosene heater had been his responsibility, a home chore assigned specially to him. He'd come home that night to find the family asleep. He'd been drunk with beer and stumbling; and sexually hung up and hurting, in the ache of his years. He'd fallen into bed in his clothes, too tangled in the snarls of himself to remember about the heater.

At the mass funeral, his Aunt Rosalina had screamed maledictions on him, and beaten him publicly. Both his cousins, Carmine and Anna, had gone to the police demanding his criminal arrest.

Father Bonnard of the Diocese had kept him in captive

prayer every day for two months. In the talks in his study, the priest had equated intoxicants and sexual license with God's wrath. He'd taken it to mean that the priest, too, believed his evil had brought doom to his father, mother, sisters and brother.

Some months later, on his seventeenth birthday, he'd taken flight, quit that Purgatory for another.

Vito suddenly cast the crucifix from him, into the debris. Resentment flickered, then flamed in his eyes, and he pouted his lips. Soon he spoke out defiantly, his voice and phrasings curiously boyish, as if he was now daring those retorts he had repressed in the time of his ordeal with his Uncle Guido, his Aunt Rosalina, his cousins and Father Bonnard. He directed his words specially at Donna somewhere, imaging her face intensely so it blurred that other one hovering in his sight, finally giving answers to his mystery; the long locked-away story at last confided in Donna, for truth and release, and so he might know compatibility with his wife in another time.

—*I was man as well as boy*, Vito related. I had this big secret! I suddenly couldn't look people in the face—not even my family. The time I tried talking about it with my cousin, that filthy Carmine turned it into a joke. At the club that night, I had to stop dancing or go crazy! Then fat-stuff Rose Pugliese was pointing a finger at it; and pretty soon, she had everybody in the club laughing with her. I ran the hell out without my coat and walked the streets for hours. Then I got cans of beer and drank them on the roof. Then at two in the morning, when I saw old Katie Shepard come rolling out of the Clover Leaf Tavern, I went up to her and told her one dollar was all I had for it—I wasn't going home every night any more, or thinking about the family—so how could I remember about the damned kerosene heater!

Vito talked more, on and on endlessly. Ranting the story he'd saved up for so long, stating it as he'd originally felt it and believed it, disavowing that guilt impressed on him, that he had mutely accepted through the long years since. Soon, as the logic of his plaint grew terribly in his mind and he began to seethe and burn with the injustice dealt him, he railed and cursed recklessly across the years. He summoned old faces before him, called them vile names and spat upon them, kicked wildly at them and pummeled them with his fists. When this fury subsided, he lay numbed and strangled for breath, afraid for what he'd done. He peered into the darkness, at black, varied forms that were looming phantoms—sure in his fears the frightful retaliation would really happen now, and swiftly.

5

The first effects Fowler experienced were familiarly like those other attacks. Spasms of pain in the chest and a feeling of suffocation, as if the heart muscle were anemic and laboring. He coughed heavily, gathering his force for it, as if blasting out fibrinous clots in the vessels.

He took a nitroglycerine tablet from the store he carried handily, and placed it under his tongue. As the original pains eased, new symptoms developed that he had no prescription for. Pricking needles now in his skull, on the right side of it and moving from back to front. His heart hammering and the sweat on him; then an arterial spasm, not so familiar as those others, which numbed and stiffened his left arm and leg as if they'd become artificial limbs.

Fowler lay in a disciplined quiet, making no outcry or appeal. He had a premonition that a final attack was coming, in the next minute or thirty—the thrombosis that was a bomb in the chest, mercifully exploding life at once.

His laugh now was just a flutter in his chest. *Death was a damned dull show,* he thought. Exciting only to watchers who saw their own faces for the dying man's, in a secret moment of masochistic fun and self-congratulation. Death was Nature at its most uncreative—the body, a hundred and ninety-five pounds of it, stuffed with steaks, chops, fruits, brandies, dissolved into a penny-count of chemicals; the brain cells storing the wealth of twenty thousand days, the billion-word catalogue of ideas, epigrams, jokes, become dead tissue.

There should be some last remarks before dying, he thought wryly. He'd perhaps been spared for a while for that—so a veteran speechmaker with memorized phrases to fit a thousand occasions could vivify his own departure.

It all tumbled in his mind now: Slum Clearance, Flag Day, Hands Across the Sea, Brotherhood Week, Mother's Day, Thanksgiving, Yuletide, Cancer, Courtesy, Creeping Socialism. He picked his way free of the debris, and devised those phrases, as true as he could make them, that he had been tempted to speak in his earlier conference with Harry Archer.

He peered out into the blackness now as if to sight Archer—for the first time acute to the havoc around him. He thrust out with an elbow and there was an immediate response of brick, plaster and glass. Horror filled him as his awareness of the enormity of the disaster grew. He thought poignantly of Lisa. How badly hurt, or was she dead? He wondered about the absolute quiet. Were they all dead? He neglected to marvel over his own immunity, the fact that he'd sustained no surface impairment he could detect. There was debris framing him, and in the aisle of his legs, arranged as if it had been placed there uncannily by hand only for the frightening picture it made.

He spoke out to Archer, or Archer's ghost. —I skipped off with a million. Hear me, Harry? A million dollars. But, Harry, I never dipped into the public till for one red cent of it. What I got away with, I was given. From time to time, I was handed little envelopes of cash—by nice fellows, with fine manners and good clothes. They'd come to my house, ask for me, then hand me a sealed envelope, with no explanation of it, no talk about it. Nothing said to personally bind me to anything, before or after the fact. Or I'd find the envelopes locked in my private desk drawer—somebody had a duplicate key. *Don't* ask me what bookkeeping decided my share of the graft, heh— I put blind trust in the invisible brain calculating it. The only time I had any conscience about it was when I got my first envelope. I'd never before seen fifteen thousand dollars in a lump—that much loot scared me. I had a small, temporary blind spot about legitimate graft and plain thievery. Heh, a problem in semantics I solved for myself pretty quick.

—You figure out for yourself who kept handing up those envelopes regularly. *I* say it was really the people; the great body of voters who'd elected me to office. Sound crazy to you, Harry? Not if you think about it logically. I was selected as nominee by party politicians, picked over a field of five. I got the nod because the consensus was that I was the most dependable front for their graft—a graft, mind you, Harry, that was an institution as traditional as Bunker Hill. It had been going on since the founding of the Republic, except possibly for a few dry spells when reformers and fanatics held temporary office.

—I say every voter with an ounce of savvy knew he was voting me in as Chief Representative of Graft, and didn't give a damn. He didn't care, and it made no difference. He understood it innately as a way of life, a necessary evil. In fact, he felt safer with me up there—a clean broom would only mean disorganization and inefficiency, everything topsy-turvy, an army of public-job holders made the butt, sacrificed to slogans. If the voter felt any emotion about me, it was envy—he'd have liked to be in my shoes!

—Now you know what I meant earlier when I said that at no time did I feel guilty of anything, at the time of that damned congressional investigation. All I could anyhow tell about under oath was the score I'd made, the million in cash I'd stashed away. Put the brand on myself; be the sacrificial goat. I didn't know a damn thing else to tell—not factually, not from knowledge. I was a beneficiary of the graft apparatus, but I wasn't part of it. Not *integrally*.

I kept my place, and wore blinkers. I acted out the role required of me, and for which I'd originally been handed that nomination: the public servant, busy with the problems of office—standing on high, clean ground, out of the muck.

There was a sudden catch in his heart, a missing beat, then a stabbing pain. As speech became difficult, Fowler breathed like a fish sucking air. —My big regret, Harry, is that the damned money's outlasted me. That I didn't get to spend every cent of it before I go.

—Even if it *was* thievery, you square everything when you fritter away the loot in the shortest possible time. Heh, pinch it from one set of consumers and give it to another set. Spread the happiness. That way, hell, what have you really gotten away with? A fling, a few kicks.

—True thievery is hoarding it. Freezing the principal and living off the interest. Never a real feedback to anybody. Like *you* do, Harry. Money's the god you pray to. It's that thing you wear in your pants!

He made mumbling sounds now, with a trembling underlip. The hard wall of darkness before him began to tilt and waver, as if the muscles that moved his eyes had become unbalanced. He closed his eyes and opened them inwardly to a kaleidoscope of pictures that showed in little bursts of exploding light. In rapid dissolves, he saw himself hardly above the ground, chubby in a white dress, standing pigeon-toed in white booties, and with golden curls to his shoulders. Then his father in an open flower-banked casket, dressed in a tuxedo and white bow tie, his cheeks streaked with rouge, and counted hairs gleaming with pomade spaced evenly and low on his forehead. Then Hugo Oelrich, his political mentor, in a straw kelly, sitting stiffly in a straight chair, with the pose reproduced eight times, front, back, and right and left profile, in as many mirrors. Then Eileen, so big and big-bottomed the stove she tended was lost to view, with the henna wig over the baldness come of childhood smallpox lopsided and ludicrously over one ear.

It stopped with Eileen, his wife for more than thirty years. Fowler wondered dimly about this odd and mystifying montage selected and reproduced by the psyche—forgotten snapshots, trivia really, in a lifetime crowded with better drama, beautiful women, vignettes and pageantry.

He conjured up his ex-wife Eileen, by voluntary will now, and tried to think of what it was he'd wanted to say to her, and for so long a time, but had never gotten around to.

Then it happened. The bomb in his chest, exploding life at once.

By the mechanism of wish, Lisa recovered Max Marsant from his tomb of dirt. She put her mouth to his, and uncannily pumped life-renewing breath into him.

She washed him clean with devoted hands, then peeled the bark of his years. He stood before her now in that sentimental portrait she kept—young as the century was young then, an esthete with the profile of male sculptures. She smoothed his fine hair, envying the natural marcel, then fluffed it so a forelock fell on his brow.

He had gifts: he'd written a poem, composed a sonata, painted a picture. He was beautiful, an *objet d'art* to collect. He made amusing talk—a marvelous partner for those nights arid of event. He lived in monkish self-prohibition —he sat among his books, or at the piano, or before his easel. He did not clamor at her, or infringe her liberty.

She'd married Max for these mere things; and because she had not yet resettled surely into herself. She'd quit the asylum hardly more than one month before. She needed a companion on call, a husband or another, to shoo the night devils.

A time later, she'd changed Max's status more valuably to father, so she would not be notoriously the bastard of Eva.

In her fantasy now, Lisa went back in time to join with Max. She stood with him, both of them young, throbbingly alive, with the adventure of countless tomorrows bulking deliciously in their minds.

They were on the Côte d'Azur, and it was 1928.

She resolved his quandary now as she had not then—or ever in their long life together. She depressed her sexual aversion for him, and crept into his bed. She gave herself elaborately to him, consummating the marriage, and giving him that definition that was the cure he needed.

A light turned on in her dark, and now Lisa saw Max's death as her own mortality: a past self of her lay buried with him. She was an old face in her mirror now, a hideous creature of camouflage, with Time's hand inexorably on her. She wept terribly, squeezing tears, as if wanting to dry out into death, hurry Time's hand.

7

A free form of beams stood in reasonable balance, as if by sculptor's plan. Janoff lay rigidly under the structure, in a bed of debris. He was bleeding from numerous wounds, skull and neck; his body was numbed, as if the total injury to it was far too extraordinary for any human reaction. His bulk rested on a flat near the hole where the floor had opened. The pit below, black and gas-choked from the broken pipes, was the cellar level where the servants were accommodated. The gas escaping the concentration in the pit stung Janoff's nose; when he became aware of the new danger, he angled his head away from the source.

He tried little wriggling movements tentatively, then heaved his shoulders and torso, twisting in a half-circle. In the sudden shifting, some debris fell away and struck hard at his body. He lay gasping now and powerless; the supreme effort had cost his residual strength. Soon now, he escaped into his own dark, pondering the materials of that world he had speculated and lost, plotting the testament he must write to rehabilitate his name and insure his immortality —the testament that would win partisans and followers who would form a world movement in his name, even posthumously, that would fuse a chain reaction of ideological explosions universally, blast Borgia from his corrupt throne of power. The hard text of it was knitted in his mind, the documented *J'Accuse* against the debauchers and heretics.

He burrowed deep into his mind now, to turn up those minor accents, the candid glimpses that were color threads in the fabric. That more clinical than political story, of the paper men behind the patent façades, of the incestuous clique bound in a brotherhood of fear, conspiracy and plunder. And each knowing the other's baseness and faults, like actors in close company when the lines had been read and the posturing was over, and the curtain dropped to illusion and audience.

He reviewed some of these homey revelations, his mind making pictures. *Bryakov*, maddened by sterility, riding his chauffeured limousine through Sochi, shooting pregnant cats and dogs through the car's side window. The sybarite *Jacob Frunze* with his exotic perfumes and closets of Parisian lingerie. Janoff's mouth wreathed in disgust—he'd once watched Frunze disport himself in the luxurious holiday house in the subtropical glade close by the Caucasian Riviera. The nose-picking *Karsky*, in his clay-colored tunic, peak cap and half-length top boots. Born Estonian, Karsky had falsified his birthplace, posing as a Georgian, so he could emulate Stalin even in this. Karsky had poisoned two wives, rid himself of a third through political denunciation. *Shustov*, with his persecution complex—high-voltage electric fences and steel-shuttered windows. Janoff smiled to himself. Shustov had a personal chef, a non-Russian deaf-mute. *Ulrich*, with his secret hoard of gold; and the obese *Floren*, with his collection of pornography that had once belonged to Hermann Goering.

Now Janoff imagined that trial he had flouted. He saw the familiar white-walled room with red damask hangings. And the platform on which sat the judges, the defendant, the public prosecutor, and the defense counsel who was no more than an abject assistant to the prosecutor. Then the small gallery high up near the ceiling, with its semicircular recess covered by heavy curtains behind which Borgia sat concealed and followed the proceedings. Emanating a greater terror because of his invisibility.

He spoke in his mind those words he must speak at the trial. Words of self-denunciation and confession, of self-abasement and penitence. With fanciful invention of that plot he had supposedly conceived and organized with enemies of the Soviet, at home and abroad. Spoken with the drug of fear in him, and with perfect acting, to satisfy the primitive peculiarities of Soviet justice, and so the public sensation would be enormous.

He'd never actually submitted to the defendant's role arranged for him by Borgia and the secret police. He'd guessed about the arrangements for him when he was ordered back to Moscow from his post in East Germany. He'd wisely stepped across the line to West Germany, then journeyed on from there. A fugitive now, with a price on his head; hunted down like a common criminal. As if he were not Georgi Stroilov who'd fought and suffered for the Revolution, in Russia, Spain, China, Czechoslovakia, as soldier, agent and statesman; who'd made speeches to congresses, who'd written flaming chapters in Party history, who'd retreated in Poland before Hitler's legions, to stand almost to the death in Stalingrad.

In flooding self-pity now, he recalled an incident forever ground into his marrow. That time only a year ago, was it? He'd been asleep in a hotel room, in the sanctuary of a neutral country. In thrashing sleep, sweating with the nightmare-imagining of tramping feet in the hall and middle-of-the-night peremptory knocks on his door. He'd suddenly jumped wide awake to find it true. Knocks on the door, and a voice with soft insinuation asking him to open the door and yield to the inevitable—a bullet in his brain. He'd gone out the back window, into the midwinter frost, shivering in his pajamas. He'd fled through strange streets to the woods, to hide in a hole with brush over it for cover and camouflage. He'd cowered there all night, his ears acute, separating the feet of stray dogs and roaming deer from those of humans, deciding tensely about the rustling of tree branches stirred up by the wind. In the first dawn, there were feet suddenly close as if walking on his head. When the dog fell through the trap, barking and thrashing in the hole, he'd strangled the beast with his last strength, and then carefully restored the brush. He'd lain taking warmth from the carcass. By full morning, with his pajamas stiff with ice and his eyes and nose running, he'd at last identified the voice at his door. *Djugash*, accredited to the Cheka, a man with eyes that lighted and dimmed like a lamp on an interrogator's desk; a psychopath, above politics, in the game for sensations, who found ecstasy in murder. He knew Djugash; in a more favorable time, he'd requisitioned the man's services.

Janoff quit his dark. The reminiscences had become too harrowing. He was beginning to despair for his project, the retaliation he so sorely wanted. He sought to return to his immediate reality. His eyes were closing in involuntary sleep, as if that inhalation of gas mixed in with air was steadily effecting its anesthesia. He bulged his eyes and fought to hold on to his faculties. He wondered vaguely about the others—how many had been killed outright, and how many were maimed, like him? He thought more sharply of Taylor, and his mouth twisted in bitterness. *We've reached the same impasse*, my American friend. Exile, and bankruptcy, our life collateral called in and forfeited. Both of us spat upon and reviled by our own multitude, and cast out.

He nodded to himself as a sudden lamp in his mind gave bolder light to his idea. *We appear different*, but we are fundamentally one, a pea that has split into twins. We act out of the anarchy in us, born in us; our varying slogans are only a device for personality, the mask behind which nihilism hides.

An old phrase stole from the limbo of his youth to his lips: *We create only to destroy*. He tried vainly to recall its source.

In the village, volunteer fire fighters with black scorched faces worked to limit the fire's spread. They were poorly equipped; there was no system of water hydrants in Choluca. The pump-driven wells were mainly unserviceable or useless in this universal emergency. There were scattered bucket brigades at several points of the stream— some groups of men, women and boys essayed pumping water from the stream until debris clogged their hoses. There was clear water, perversely, bubbling and flowing here and there in wide wounds in the street, where the streams had been underground.

On the Avenida Maria Cristina, a wine merchant and his remnant factory crew were recklessly hurling buckets of wine on encroaching flames that threatened the low-storied frame winery.

In a sanctuary on the southeast boundary still untouched by flames, a pickup crew of dynamiters, ten in number, were wrangling over a project for breaking the fire in its onward path, by blowing up rows of buildings one or two blocks deep and thus creating a broad open space. They had a half-ton of guncotton in fortunate supply, warehoused and forgotten for almost a year by a road-building company faced with the problem of blasting through rock mountains. There were no skilled engineers in the rabble group, and none of the men knew the science of handling explosives. The acrimonious debate had to do mainly with where to place the explosive—the men could not agree on any area of the village that might be expendable for the greater good.

Looting had begun, and in the absence of soldiers and police the haggard-eyed owners of shops and costly homes and their relatives formed into armed vigilante corps, each patrolling his own property despite the furnacelike heat. There was a high number of shootings, as the owners by silent declaration ruled their square of property to be eminent domain, with trespass punishable by summary execution.

In La Avenida Oriente, where the library and public school were, four men working in relays were dumping armloads of books on a horseless wagon. A fifth man, too aged to work, clutched an illuminated Bible to his breast. When the wagon was loaded, while the aged man rode the tail gate, the four pulled the wagon, two at each shaft, to higher, temporarily safer ground.

Father Porfirio still tirelessly roamed the streets, with his teeth and spirit set against the pain in him, in the cart wheeled loyally by Joachim. His face was dirt-caked and his clothes torn; the silk band that was the eucharistic vestment worn over his left forearm hung in tatters. When certain passing refugees offered him precious water and drink from bottles and canteens they carried hidden in their clothes, Father Porfirio refused it. When the village physician, Lázaro Avila, offered to devise wood supports for his broken legs and otherwise treat him, Father Porfirio argued that it would have to wait until a freer time. When a *curandero* offered to perform a special ritual that would restore Father Porfirio, the priest loudly upbraided the witch doctor and called him a faker. When Father Porfirio spied an Indian in an alley staggering under the weight of a sack, he ordered Joachim to seize the man and search the sack. Joachim opened the knots in the sack and then dumped out better than a hundred pounds of treasure: candelabra, clocks, *objets d'art* and silver. When the Indian, whose clothes were ragged, brazenly protested that he was salvaging his own belongings, the priest confiscated the loot and ordered the man to Confession on the spot. The Indian squirmed rebelliously until Joachim laid on with his stick.

Later, stationed perilously by the division where the northeast wind so far saved one-half of the village from burning, Father Porfirio humped reflectively in his cart, with his round cheeks ruddy and tanned by the refraction of lights that were red spirals of flame. Soon he ordered Joachim to round up a quorum of the faithful. In a while, with more than a score of people gathered around his cart, Father Porfirio bade them kneel, faces hard to the flaming sector of Choluca, and send up mass prayers for rain.

When the mass prayers were over, Father Porfirio read aloud from Revelation, Chapter XX, beginning with verse 12: " 'And I saw the dead, small and great, stand before God; and the books were opened: and another book was opened, which is the book of life: and the dead were judged out of those things which were written in the books, according to their works. And the sea gave up the dead which were in it; and death and hell delivered up the dead which were in them: and they were judged every man according to their works. And death and hell were cast into the lake of fire. This is the second death. And whosoever was not found written in the book of life was cast into the lake of fire.' "

9

Taylor's eyes fluttered open. There was a still-damp paste on his eyelashes, as if his eyes had cried during his sleep. A sleep in which he had journeyed through dark labyrinths and recesses of memory. He was seething inside—a confused, inexpressible hatred more than he could abide, prone and helpless as he was now. He ached for movement, and forms before him that he could assault. Some sensation had returned to his lower half; he could flex his knees now, throw one leg over the other. The hell in his rib cage wrote its own diagnosis: broken ribs, a good many of them.

He stared hot-eyed into the blackness, driven to rant at the top of his voice—break with this sick, subjective, inarticulate trysting with the night. Words were his expression, the essence of personality; he was whole only so long as he talked. Words born of his heat, with value only accessory to them. The thing was the rage and the intoxi-cating sense of target, how his weapons fared in battle. This was that truth transcending all others; the ceaseless attack, attack, attack, the epithetical scourging of the Smugs, a candid mirror held so it stripped man naked and showed him his bestiality.

This was his role, the meaning of his life—he was a roving dynamiter blowing up all ghettos of the mind. So a new breed could forge a new faith, make the first primitive tool, build the first house, labor in a new day unfettered by yesterday.

Taylor made savage nod to it. Yesterday was the shadow over today, blotting out the sun. Twentieth-century man lived merely as caretaker of the museum-past, the two thousand years of it; and moldering above the earth as his ancestors moldered beneath.

When Taylor did speak out, he thought strangely that he was *not* hearing himself. That someone else was mys-teriously speaking through him, using him as a vehicle. The voice was sober and restrained, heavy with discovery, as if that stranger had journeyed right along with him through those dark recesses, observing, interpreting and taking down notes. The words said were naïve, not at all Taylor; as small as man in feeling and scope, embarrass-ingly human, odious to his ears. He tried helplessly to expel his tenant, stop the banal solemnities being put forth in his name.

—Helga *really* died at the Ebro with that young cap-tain. To serve Helga's wants, and save her, I'd have had to concede the wanton nature of the first murder. I could no longer justify it as an act of political faith.

—My faith was shaken twice, and then it hardened again. Helga'd made two earlier attempts on her life—first when the butcher made that public scene, accusing her of murdering his son in Korea, and then a second time when my son Michael was brutally beaten by his classmates.

—I could not do the expedient thing, *or* the convenient thing. *My* life was at stake too—the logic of all my years. I had to be whole, really and consistently, or become nothing. Pull one basic thread, and the cloth unravels . . .

—I knew Helga would try again to take her life, that night those guests sneaked into our house using the rear door. I saw Helga's plan in her face, when she excused herself, then locked herself in the bathroom. I knew by the count of time that she lay dying in the bathroom, but there was nothing I could do.

—There was nothing I *wanted* to do. Helga asked too high a price from me for her life—more than I could pay.

—*Two* murders for one. *One* immutable logic. I shot the young captain, and by that, poisoned Helga across the years.

—Who judges me? Who *dares* . . .

10

Harding lay pinioned as if in medieval stocks. His upper body was free, it felt hardly more than bruised—he could move his hands, arms, shoulders and head. He was winded, as if the return to consciousness had been a long, slow, uphill climb from the bowels of the earth. His mind was empty, a blank slate, with the moment of his whereabouts and even memory erased. He lay in a refuge that was the capricious result of the earth paroxysm and shifting masonry. He was in a salon apart from the great, main one; the dividing wall that had been was moved as if it had been set on rollers to shrink the space of this salon into a closet. This wall balanced against another one now, in an almost perfect tilt, making an odd-shaped cave with head room hardly enough for a standing man. Three sides of the cave were windowless, sealed to light, air, view, like a mausoleum, the fourth side looked out telescopically into the blackness. The sights through this were only to be seen imaginatively—there were patterns and blockades of wreckage as if running into infinity.

The cave was extraordinarily free of debris, as if the wall had moved on the rollers to fashion its redoubt first, and then the assaulting chunks of stone, steel, wood and objects had battered against it. The exact construction of the cave made Harding's own plight seem freakish; the source of those beams pinioning him was mysterious; they visibly could not have been abstracted from the form of the refuge.

The mind's restoration happened slowly—buttons of light flickering distantly in the black morass of his time. And in each light, separately, he saw himself, forgotten faces of himself, and some of them loathsome. As if the first need of the mind was perversely the establishing of ordinary identity, the sheer fact of him proved alive and abroad on earth. Soon now, as recovery accelerated, the lights brightened and incidents imposed over his face, played vividly for him in the eye. He saw scenes that were tolerably himself in passage, his healthy self; and then those scenes that were intolerably his other self, the one locked away in secret, exposed only in that hour of pain and panic on the psychoanalyst's couch.

He groped back to the *now* of Choluca and the destroyed Villa de la Soledad, by reversing time so that he was on the plane again, destination Mexico City, then in the limousine chauffeured by Rufino on the Pan-American Highway. He dallied in Choluca village more than he really had those hours before, more occupied with it now than then, even enjoying it more, as if prescient this time about the catastrophe to come and seeking to delay the horror of it.

Soon enough, total awareness of his whereabouts and plight settled heavily into his mind. He made a brief testing of the weights imprisoning his legs, shanks and buttocks. They were beyond his power to move or dislodge. He put his palms flat on the floor and tried ineffectually to raise up. He could barely half-sit, maintained up to his strength by the support of his arms, with a tension in the curve of his back that threatened to splinter his spine. He sank back, to lie horizontal and inert. He keyed his hearing to sound now, concentrating every sense into this one until his ears ached with it. He heard breathing, harsh and rattling—someone was in acute distress. He listened again, very carefully, to gauge the distance of the breather from him. Then, soon, it was louder in his ears; he could almost feel the pumping of breath touch his cheek.

Close—he decided about it. There's somebody lying close to me as if we were two in a bed, parted by the merest corridor of space.

He reached out now to touch the form beside him—his hand reacting sensitively to the unusual body heat he felt. He traced the outline of a thigh, soft and womanly, then over to the rubber-hard ball that was the belly.

The name *Susan* was on his lips, but he said *Donna* in his mind. The obvious pregnancy identified her unmistakably.

Donna's hand responded to his and she grasped his fingers urgently, signaling the distress that was so telltale in her breathing. When he tried to free his hand, she clutched it even more desperately.

"Señor, please help me," she said in fevered tones. "Please help me not to faint. It will be bad if I faint."

He was puzzling the oddity of this when she said, "I have no pain from the earthquake, Señor. I am only having my baby. Señor, I feel I am now having my baby!"

He felt her nails in his hand, sharp as spears.

"I can't be of any help," Harding said wretchedly. "I'm in a damned vise from the waist down." He squeezed her hand hard now, as if transfusing strength.

She wriggled on her back and buttocks; soon lay close beside him, breathing harshly, her legs crossed and her body contracted.

Harding asked anxiously, "Do you know what to do?" He had a wild impulse to beg her to please postpone the event, wait for a more fortunate time and setting.

"I have had a baby once before," she replied gaspingly. "My son, Domingo. I know what to do." Some moments later, she said as if assuring herself, "In my village, I have watched it many times. With another woman to help the mother, and sometimes only a child. *Sí*, yes, I know what to do."

Her speech quieted some of the panic swelling in him; eased the pain in his groin that was a cutting knife.

Harding felt in a pocket, found a handkerchief, then twisted to pat her brow and cheeks dry. She bit at the handkerchief with strong teeth, and he knew to make a roll of it and leave it there. In a while, he remembered about the small, cylindrical flashlight he kept attached to his key ring. He shone the pencil of light on her tumultuous chest, the constriction of neck and cheek muscles, the rolled handkerchief between her teeth. She looked big, a great mold of woman bursting from doll's clothes that were hardly any cover. The beam held on her face and her eyes glinted a smile, as if her sense about it was that he needed the reassurance.

He beamed his light beyond Donna now, exploring the limits of the cave they were in. There was a powdery dust hanging in the air—the weak light he shone flattened against it as if it were a wall. He trained it down on the floor, far as the beam would carry. It made an irregular yellow stain like a splash of paint. Through strain-

225

ing sight, he saw a shoe pointing like an arrow. His hand shook violently, and the beam wavered so the focus was lost. He tried finding it again, but the power of the flashlight battery was cut now, so that the beam fell short.

He began to sweat as if water were running from his pores. *Susan's shoe*, he told himself fearfully. He screamed her name now with an awful tension of cords in his throat—*Susan, Susan, Susan* . . .

There was no reply, only his own voice. He lay dumbly now, cold as if pressed between blocks of ice; and not daring his thoughts, wanting not to think.

11

She'd heard her name called, distant and echoing eerily as in a dream. When Harding stopped his cries, Susan stared out into the blackness where the pinhead of yellow light had danced, and where she knew him to be. She tried her voice again, forcing sound through the knots and ties in her throat. She made whimpering noises, and then a sharp, thin blade of sound that was an *E-eeeeeee*. She kept on with it, as if she were doing exercises, and soon she could talk in her mouth.

She was lying rigidly on her side, in shock, a straight line from head to feet. One arm was raised high in a curious declamatory gesture, with the fingers parted. She kept the arm aloft remarkably long, for the endurance it required.

In the activity of her mind, she was still on that ground-level patio with Harding in the lowering dusk, as if there'd been no separation of time, no event of earthquake. The sequence played for her, full of its bravado, speech and revelation, but now also with that text supplied to it that had only been hinted before and finally evaded.

She saw the narrow screen where the roads formed a T at their juncture, saw the native folk, young and old, and their animals and livestock, march across the screen in a procession of pictures. There was the scent of jasmine heady in her senses, and that feeling back in her of bonds and being caged and wanting space terribly.

She came eye to eye with Harding now, and at last dared say those things that had first been only implied. Her lost voice was back, clear and true, cured at once, as if what perhaps had muted it in shock were those un-spoken thoughts that lay stagnant and festering in her mind and blood.

—*Bales of dirty laundry*, Richard. We've more than anybody—it's our greatest harvest! It's filled our house, evicted us from every room, and from our life with each other. And how . . . do you ever launder such an accumulation?

—You see, I've known for a long time why you were always so enraged at Doobs. Why you spoke of him to me in the vilest words, and always impugning his manhood—that Doobs was hardly a man. I understood that it was more than just the wrangling and ego competition in your agency operation. I knew the truth of it intuitively, as a woman is aware of love and hate; and then, later, I knew it shatteringly, when I appealed to your Doctor Barshak. When I found you'd given him up, I felt really hopeless, despondent for our marriage—that it would go on as it had been. I'd live as your companion, keeper of the retreat you came to when in flight from yourself.

—When you kissed me, it was seldom on the mouth. In an embrace, you were gentlemanly, never touching me suggestively, careful not to excite me. I slept alone so soon after our honeymoon; when you took me to bed, you first drank for hours, as if it was impossible to make love to me in a sober condition. And then, in the sex act, I wasn't your wife, but a whore to be used in violence.

—I left for Mexico certain I finally wanted a divorce, after that last company party at the Park Lane. You were in high spirits at the party, beaming at everybody, and so affectionate with Doobs. As if you two had patched something up and you were having your own celebration. I sat among the wives over cocktails, watching you act out your feelings with Doobs.

—*And my own laundry*. A car passing Balfour's did stop that day of my thirty-eighth birthday. A cheaper car, a Plymouth with broken fenders and a man in it with grubby cheeks who wore a workman's cap. We drove in silence for some miles, with no exchange of introductions. Then he said I was pretty in my dress and I reminded him of Ava Gardner in the movies. When I knew I couldn't go through with it and asked to be let off at the Crescent Ridge taxi stand, he drove up a side road, and parked. He forced me into the back seat and attacked me. There was something pressing into my back; later I saw it was a child's toy, a red-and-blue tow truck. He finally drove me to the Crescent Ridge taxi stand, and smiled and tipped his cap when I stood on the walk. I've seen his mouth in my nightmares ever since. He had a broken upper bridge that hung loosely in his mouth.

—In a month, I found myself pregnant. It took a workman to accomplish it, and in so few minutes! I had the abortion done in Havana, that time you thought I was visiting Harvey and Fran. A Cuban doctor who kept pictures of his five grandchildren on his desk. He persuaded me to think it over for twenty-four hours, discuss it further with my husband, perhaps redecide it and have the baby. I wasn't so young, he said; time and my prospects for motherhood were running out!

12

Harding first wept silently, and then as the stabbing ache in his breast became unbearable and he filled up with pity for himself and Susan, the eye of his pity mainly for Susan, his body shook and he yielded to uncontrolled bursts of weeping.

In a while, he lay exhausted, not crying any more, with his eyes red and swollen and his chest hurting, and the depth of his pity for Susan now even more profound—he was moved for her with a force of emotion new to him. He spoke chaotically in his mind, in a dialogue with Susan, giving answers, attempting to explain things about himself, what had burdened and driven him, the passions and confusions in him seeded in boyhood and grown malignantly that had been the evil of their marriage.

He heard Donna say practically, in a tone that condoned what she had overheard, "Be happy she is not dead. Nor you, Señor. There is always time to fix your life, if you are alive." She touched his cheek lingeringly, in a sign of compassion for him, then suddenly closed her hand into a fist as the pain began to come faster.

Harding said anxiously, "How is it?"

"Better now, Señor," she gasped. "Now that I am having my baby." She added, "This time the sac did not break, like with Domingo. *Dios*, I could not stand a dry birth!"

He lay aware of her flesh and her boiling heat. After some time, he asked tensely, "Is it all right?"

"*Sí*, yes," she replied. "The head is down, is outside. Señor, please take my hand!"

He held her hand, throbbing with her rhythmic contractions, in staring terror of the next crisis, when an infant would be born.

Donna said suddenly, "Two strips from your shirt, Señor—or tear the handkerchief. To tie the cord in two places. And if you have a knife, something that will cut?"

He obeyed fumblingly; he tore at his shirt, ripping up so the buttons flew and stung his face. He was some time getting the knife off his key ring; a longer time finding that groove that was the knife in the complex tooling of corkscrew, bottle opener, nail file.

Harding passed the strips of cloth and the knife to her. He lay now with a swelling heart, speculating on her activity—what exactly did Donna have to do?

Working rapidly, Donna tied the umbilical cord tightly in two places, to divide the placenta from the baby. Then, using the knife blade, she competently cut in between, close to the navel of the infant, freeing it from its connection to her. This done, she raised the infant and laid it face down on her belly. She lay very still now, seeking reserves of breath and waiting for the afterbirth to thrombose.

Soon there was the cry of newborn life.

Harding beamed his flashlight at Donna; on her dark eyes and hair, the prominent mold of her breasts. He noted the creature lying naked and face down on her immensity. He stared at it intensely, and soon jealously, coveting the great cushions and the warm fires of the mother. Another picture injected itself before him, haunting him now as it had haunted his years. *His own mother*, fragile and wispy, so elusive to his senses he could only realize her by eye, like a delicate painting. He kept on staring down, until both forms blurred into one, the brown one with its stores of food and love, and the other one that was frail and milk-dry and queerly boylike.

Harding wrenched his eyes away guiltily, and back up to Donna's face. Her eyes flicked open and she looked at him strangely, as if she had forgotten him. "It was the cry of a son," she said softly, as if to herself. "I have a second son now."

13

The phrase stayed repetitiously on Janoff's lips, as if this were the thread by which he clung to life. *We create only to destroy.* He kept thinking it and saying it, oddly as if counting time by it—his tongue a pendulum in his big clock of a head. As his senses waned and his surety of death became acute, he shrilled the phrase that was nagging him to the last—*We create only to* . . .

He conjured up Alec Taylor, Taylor as he'd been before at the bar, hard-eyed and relentless, orating at the group. Taylor cravenly serving Borgia; speaking in a high voice so his words would carry to Borgia where he sat behind heavy curtains in the heights. In Janoff's eye now, Taylor's face dropped as if it were a mask worn over other masks. The face now was the public prosecutor Drobny; then as masks kept falling, the faces were in turn Bryakov, Jacob Frunze, Karsky, and finally the assassin Djugash.

Janoff screamed into the blackness, "Party scum. You, *Taylor,* hear me. I command you to hear me!" He listened to the silence for a while. "Come, you've taken commands from me before. This is Georgi Stroilov, your Party god. Selected by Stalin himself to stand publicly fifth from his right. *American Communist*, hear me—I've ordered your life!"

He listened to the hard silence again, and decided that Taylor was dead. He marshaled what remaining voice he had—"*I'll then write your epitaph!*" He made his words purposely ornate, and spoke them deliberately, as if they were to be of lasting record: "*Dupe*, altar boy, fool of the ages. We joked about you and made dirty anecdotes—your ears would burn! You made our book a bible, and the Party a tabernacle—the Cause was a new religion, its masters new gods for that one you had forsaken. Your piety embarrassed and sickened us. You were more the enemy than anybody because you lived in our house, mimicked our words, stamped your sacrifices with our name. We had to be careful—wear God's face for you, the lot of us. We were made to speak in two voices: one voice for you, and the other among ourselves. And always the worry—that the starry long view would fall to the day-by-day reality. That you would finally see the Revolution nonideally and really, and be shocked and outraged."

Janoff lay in self-enforced silence now. Frightened by what he was thinking, the trend of his speech. As if his polemic directed at the image of Taylor had opened a certain vein, and in the next spilling there would be self-excoriation, the eye of accusation turned against himself. As his inner torment kept up, it flashed through him that the book he would write from memory and emotion and the valise-ful of papers and memoranda he'd carried across the world, could never serve him with posterity, or win any honor. That it would degrade him with the others, expose him even as it exposed them. That he was one with them, a blood brother, as guilty as they, even though now an outsider.

This thinking now leavened his despondency over the unwritten book. The earthquake had been fate's intervention—his hand and brain prevented from an act that would only damn him in the world mind, now and all through time. Damage that legend and his posture in after-history even more shatteringly than the machinations of Borgia and his acolytes had already done.

Truth was for fools and weaklings—anathema to a superior man whose life doctrine was *Realpolitik*. The testament could only be a confession; and maudlin and pathetic as the last-words candor of a sinner, faker or criminal. No book, of course! Georgi Stroilov would endure wrapped in enigma for a thousand years—a hero to some, a whelp to others, imagined, idealized, case-psychologized, vilified, researched by historians; his personality, ideas and deeds pieced together from scraps of paper, records, apocrypha, the memories of man. He would watch the nonsense from a cloud of his choice—he would laugh all through eternity.

Janoff's mouth opened wide and his eyes bulged, as if that moment had arrived. When time passed, and he found he was still alive, although barely, he began to act peculiarly. He changed the angle of his head, and looked suspiciously into the blackness. His eyes darted to and fro, as if the darkness were an ambush, and the shapes and forms in his sight were avengers about to spring upon him. Soon now, the recurrent fear possessed him once more—that death would be administered to him; that he would be murdered.

234

Murdered—Janoff said the word to himself fatefully and ironically. Even yet, already dying as he was; and here, in a house of dead.

His eyes touched every black shape and form singly now, his ears straining to catch the least sound of movement in the ruins. Then he opened the shell of the massive gold ring he wore, took a pellet from the hollow and held it in his hand ready to his tongue. *One minute*—he remembered the old instructions about the almost instant fatality of the poison.

14

Taylor crept along the floor, using his elbows as stays, then thrusting forward from his hips. After each single movement he stopped, writhing and fainting with the agony in his rib cage. His hands were cut and broken from the passage over glass and sharp-edged debris; one side of his face was torn where he'd propelled forward head-first into a hill of debris.

He revived from a fainting spell, his third so far, with his mind nebulous. What had impelled him to fury and movement? He raised up on his elbows and stared out as if his eyes were torches and somewhere in the blackness there were some clue to the missing thought.

He listened intensely, his ears great sucking vacuums gathering in the faintest after-echoes of sound. *Yes*—it suddenly came back to him. The speech he'd heard, and his name called. *But*—he was filled with doubt about it now— had he really heard the fellow? Or were the words only imagined, spoken in his own mind?

He moved forward again, even more slowly now. Crawling inch by inch, dragging his useless legs, one hand out first cautiously, feeling for obstacles and threatening hills of debris.

It took interminably long, and soon he had the sensation that there was a tilt to the flat of the floor, that he was moving down a slope, down into an abyss. As his dis-equilibrium intensified and the tilt became sheer and perpendicular, his hand clutched at the darkness, wanting something to hold on to for support. When he felt substance hard to his fingers, he clawed deeply into it, seizing at it with both hands.

He felt he was dangling in space, and then head over heels, in eternal downward flight that had no stop. And his senses spilling from him, like an emptying of pockets, and his accumulation irretrievably lost in the limitless corners of the great void.

He heard the voice closely; words borne on breath into his ear—"*I die as my own executioner, Taylor. It will be proved that you strangled a man who first murdered himself. My victory!*"

Taylor freed one hand to feel over the surface he clutched. He traced the face with his fingers; brow, eyes, nose, the chin that was one with the neck, organizing them so they made a picture for him. He retouched the picture with invention born of memory, so that he now saw Gómez with heavy mustaches in a uniform of rank. Then Gómez become Rotha again: champagne-sotted, with loose, steaming cheeks, the mustache gone, the hair cropped close and dyed tomato-red.

He neglected to ask the question, even crucial and personal to him as it was. *Were you once Gómez, then Rotha? That time a thousand years ago at the Ebro just before the retreat—in the wine cellar in Catalonia?*

Instead he said the consistent thing, so the whole of his life would not be absurd, filling every crack in his self-image, making it hard and true and final.

Traitor—Taylor's fingers bore into the throat he held. He had this stability now, a supreme moment of self with the earth once more hard under him.

At that summit of ecstasy, the earth fell away again, and the fall that had no stop resumed. He held Stroilov tightly in the downward flight, as if his flesh itself had resolved not to lose *this* possession to the void.

The free form of beams that raised over Janoff shifted and then toppled as the violence at the base jarred the uneasy balance of the structure. One beam struck squarely at Taylor, as if uncannily aimed, and with deadly force.

15

She saw it first as Max's last painting—the half-circle of seated male nudes, with the first one callowly young, and the last one massive, sitting in a tub of flesh. Then as dreadful images of her own altered their looks they became leering night devils, transparent, bodiless, each one of them alternatingly male and female, with desiccated, senile faces. As her eye animated them, they whirled about in erotic dances, in a theater privately for her.

She screamed frenziedly for Eva, and then for Leona, and then for Max, to come and shoo the night devils. Her symptoms were the same old ones: sweating and faintness, and a sensation of heat in the abdomen.

She lay docilely after a while, knowing in a fathom of her that this was that juncture when her needs would finally be tended. That fine, skillful hands would soothe her, transfuse to her calm and the longest sleep. That she would be secured and secure.

As in Cannes once. And another time—what was the name of that lovely island of roses?

16

It began to rain some time after midnight. First a light, teasing rain, then great drops that crackled and steamed striking the ground. With this, there was rolling thunder, then thunderclaps, heralding the deluging downpour that was unprecedented in dry and arid Choluca.

The thirsty sufferers lay on the ground, faces to the sky, screaming frenzied hallelujahs with their mouths open greedily to the rainwater. Under the impact of the millions of tons of drenching water the great blazing fires became steadily smaller, deteriorating into scattered eddies of flame slowly dying out.

Father Porfirio set up a temporary altar in the shell of a house adjacent to the rubble of the Church San Felipe. The altar was lighted by a solitary candle; on a mud-stained wall the priest hung pictures of the Immaculate Conception, the Crucifixion and the Virgin Mary that he'd made Joachim salvage from the ruins of the church. The priest's movements were now enfeebled as his life force waned. The infection in his broken legs had turned gangrenous; he was running a high, killing fever.

By pre-dawn, the rain stopped, and voluntary squads of townspeople began the enormous job of clearing streets, making passages through the ruins, leveling dangerous structures.

Help came now from the outside, from Mexico City and from neighboring United States. First a trickling, helicopters and jeeps carrying medical and engineering personnel, food, medicines, machinery and technical supplies for demolition work; and then, with full morning, help arrived more equal in size and organization to the crisis.

The in-coming corps of rescuers found a good half of Choluca a bleak, level desert with craters of mud and piles of blackened brick and wood, and here and there lines of dead and leafless shrubbery.

Engineers now took charge of the voluntary squads. They organized the human rescue, worked to restore communications, made detailed surveys of the ruins, devised first-aid for buildings that could be saved, rationalized the disposal of debris, chose the sites that were to be community rubble dumps.

Stalls were set up in numerous places for the issuance of food and other necessities. Bivouacs of matting, planks and sailcloth appeared in the high, open spaces, functioning as emergency shelters and field hospitals. Medical teams moved down lines of people giving typhoid shots. Some of the critically ill were flown out, or moved by ambulance-jeep, to hospitals in other areas and in nearby Mexico City. The unmanageable insane were rounded up by soldiers and temporarily herded into a blockhouse that had sustained only partial damage. After some words between the health officers and leading Cholucans, a plan for the quickest disposal of the charrred and mutilated dead bodies was agreed to. The cadavers were brought to a designated area, put in a pile and set on fire.

Rescue squads, working north and west from Avenida San Nicolás to the heights, reached the Villa de la Soledad at 8:00 A.M. By advice of the supervising engineer, workmen wielding spades and pickaxes cleared a path to the low-level easterly wing of the villa where the servants had been quartered. When the gray-pebbled-mortar retaining wall was finally exposed, they first shored it up with planks of heavy wood, and then they tooled and gouged into the wall, creating a square wide enough for the passage of a human body.

In the gas-choked basement, searchers found the lifeless bodies of three native women and an infant. The corpses were unmarked, with no visible physical injuries—natural in death except for that puffiness to their cheeks and eyes caused by gas asphyxiation.

After a futile search for stairs and doors, a way was devised for getting upstairs to the salons. The men formed a human ladder: one man below, bearing the weight of those aloft.

They found the ground-level dank; cryptlike in the freakish divisions of space wrought by the earthquake. The three searchers abroad in the salons clung together as if that death that had struck the Villa de la Soledad still stalked the ruins. They moved in time with each other and their bodies touching, stepping carefully with the beam of the large, battery-powered light one of them carried.

They spied Alec Taylor first—a beam through his skull so his mouth and jaw hung slack, shaped everlastingly in a hideous grin. They saw the talon-spread of fingers like arrows guiding their beam to Janoff. They stared now from Taylor to Janoff, interpreting the figure of assault they saw, and wondering about the story of it.

They were moving away into other recesses, careful

first to assure their ground by using the beamed light, when they heard the wailing of an infant. When they knew the cries had come from behind impassable barriers, they returned to the basement to make their report.

In good time, more men joined with the few stymied by the formidable requirements of the Villa de la Soledad. They brought their best equipment to the task, now seeking to tunnel through the landslide of rocks and earth that formed a sealing wall around the villa proper, north, west and south.

By midafternoon, a path, secured by scaffolding and an improvised dam of rocks, ran thirty feet to the crumbled north wall of the villa. Inside the heaping ruins of the villa now, men carrying shovels, pickaxes, stretchers and body bags formed teams of two and three, fanning out to explore methodically the immensity of the villa.

17

The native officer in command gave the order again. Overtired as he was, with his vision blurry so that his men all looked alike to him, he'd taken to giving the same order at intervals. That all foreigners, when feasible and facilities permitting, would at once be evacuated to Mexico City. Said varyingly in Spanish and English, as if simultaneously to instruct his troops and reassure that queue of foreigners within earshot.

Harding lay lathered in sweat on the ground beside the helicopter, where the stretcher-bearers had temporarily set him. He heard the echoing blasts of the dynamiting, and watched a flock of birds panic and flap desperately in a vertical climb until they were lost behind low-lying clouds. Soon, from a corner of his eye, he saw the round thighs and flesh of Donna Flores as her skirts blew while she was being lifted into the helicopter by two soldiers. He listened anxiously now with a lumping throat, and then when he heard the demanding cries, he smiled happily in the knowledge that the baby was fine and clasped in its mother's arms. He angled his head slightly, better to observe the loading of the helicopter. He read the upside-down lettering on the side of the machine as United States Army with a start of surprise and an involuntary welling of tears. He watched a stretcher, with the mold of a backside bulging the brown canvas, raise slowly, then disappear over the side of the helicopter. *Vito Avedon*—he said the name gladly to himself. The boy would have a father, too!

He heard feet shuffling closer, and as if warned by some extra sense, he shut his eyes tightly to the next transfer of human cargo. He'd already seen Lisa Franke in her plight when he'd been carried through the streets, and it was more than he could bear. A gibbering madwoman with animal teeth; for lack of a strait jacket trussed crudely with rope on her arms, body, legs, and a gag in her mouth. He heard

243

the soldiers grunt, heaving the ungiving weight of her, and then mutter epithets in their native tongue.

He quailed now, remembering the other horrors he had glimpsed on the way down from the villa to the make-shift air strip. He tried to project away from Choluca, to another time and place; tomorrow after tomorrow wonderfully in New York City, with the tragedy and the stricken village half-real in his memory, a bad dream, too incredible, anyhow in limbo. But the theme of death bulked stubbornly in his thoughts, and he tolled off the names of those he knew about. *Not Susan*, he assured himself first and quickly, with swelling gladness. He'd glimpsed her on one of the paths, walking between two Red Cross workers as if learning her first steps. *Then* Ed Fowler, Archer, Taylor, Janoff, Hertzig. *No*, not Hertzig —from what he'd been able to gather, the producer so far hadn't been found, dead or alive.

He *wished* Hertzig alive now—conferring this gift from the store of his own good luck. *Funny little fellow, Hertzig*, he thought indulgently. Not a bad sort, all in all. The trouble with Hertzig was that damned defensiveness, the legacy passed along by two thousand years of ancestors. Otherwise . . .

Hertzig *was* alive—Harding made a bet with himself. The Hertzigs, right down through time, had an uncanny knack for survival.

There was a hiatus in the loading now. He could hear the Requiem Mass, funereal and haunting the air. He tried to deaden himself against the sticky-sweet odor that blew down to the hub from the one continuing fire in the heights. A sadness filled him, and he resolved to make a contribution to human relief and the rebuilding of Choluca. He wrote out the check in his mind, and then impulsively added a fourth zero to the sum. He thought suddenly of Rufino outside the Casa Cámara—God, was it only yesterday? The chauffeur flushed with drink and grinning foolishly, jiggling the toy skeleton pinned to his coat lapel. He made a note in his mind to inquire about Rufino first chance, at the automobile rental agency in Mexico City. *If it develops that Rufino was either disabled or killed*—Harding made a solemn promise to himself: A substantial check goes to the chauffeur's family, even if I have to go deeper into hock.

A pair of soldiers moved Harding some yards, to the ground beside a second helicopter. He asked questions about it, then shook his head ignorantly when they replied in Spanish. In minutes now, the first helicopter took off, rising in his sight as if drawn straight up by invisible cords.

Soon he was first to be placed in the other helicopter. He lay on the floor in the aisle for sullen minutes, lonely in the web of it, with only a patch of sky in his eye now. Then the next in turn was helped aboard and he saw it was Susan—her hair disheveled, a luster of fever in her eyes; and startlingly smaller and shriveled, as if she had dehydrated during the long night.

She sat over him, an arm's length away. They stared at each other, communicating without sound, only moving their lips. He made light of his condition, assuring her that he'd be fine quick as quick. She made assurances in kind about herself, drawing a circle around them as if they were two alone, sheltering in an alien world. They smiled to each other, the warming smiles of old, old acquaintances.

ABOUT THE AUTHORS

If anyone should ask MILTON BERLE why he waited until now to write a novel, he is one of the few people in the world who have the right to answer, "I didn't have the time." Berle has been constantly busy as an entertainer since the age of five, when he made his film debut in Marie Dressler's film, *Tillie's Punctured Romance*. He played many other film roles as a child, most of them straight dramatic parts. His talent as a comedian was first recognized when his imitation of Charlie Chaplin won him first prize in a local amateur contest. He played his first professional stage role on March 29, 1920, in the Shuberts' revival of *Floradora*. Berle got his first chance as a comedian in vaudeville; after that, he was on his way to the big time in that field, and later in theater, night clubs, song-writing, radio and television. The first big-name personality to break into TV, Berle was acclaimed as "Mr. Television" in 1948, when his program scored the highest survey rating ever reported for a regularly scheduled radio or TV show. In addition to his many professional activities, Berle has found time to raise large sums of money for worthy causes by playing benefit performances.

Born in New York City, Milton Berle attended public schools before he entered the Professional Children's School.

During his early career, his mother, the late Sandra Berle, was his guide, inspiration and one-woman claque. She remained an important influence on his career and in his life, until her death in 1954 at the age of seventy-seven.

If JOHN ROEBURT'S twelve books were all he had written, he would have made his mark on the literary scene. The fact that he has made substantial contributions to nearly every area of writing stamps him as one of the most versatile authors working today. Let's look at the record: night-police-court reporting, propaganda analyses, lectures in journalism and creative writing; noted racket exposés for such magazines as *Esquire, American Mercury, Pageant;* more than seven hundred radio and television dramas for all the major networks, including such shows as Inner Sanctum, the Kate Smith Hour, the William Gargan show, the Joseph Cotten show, and scores of others; a group of motion pictures for United Artists release; documentaries such as the Civil Defense Show and the United Jewish Appeal program. His twelve books include *Seneca USA,* a selection of the Jewish Book Guild, *The Lunatic Time,* and *The Hollow Man.* In reviewing his most recent novel, *The Climate of Hell,* the celebrated British magazine *Punch* characterized Roeburt as "a powerful new   "